BATTLE WITHOUT HONOR OR HUMANITY
VOLUME 1

BATTLE WITHOUT HONOR OR HUMANITY
VOLUME 1
DISCOMBOBULATE & NEUTRALIZE

D. HARLAN WILSON

RAW DOG SCREAMING PRESS

PRAISE FOR THE WORK OF D. HARLAN WILSON

"Provocative entertainment."
—*Booklist*

"A bludgeoning celluloid rush of language and ideas served from an action-painter's bucket of fluorescent spatter."
—Alan Moore

"New bursts of stream-of-cyberconsciousness prose."
—*Library Journal*

"Wilson writes with the crazed precision of a futuristic war machine gone rogue."
—Lavie Tidhar

"Wacky experimental fiction."
—*Publishers Weekly*

"Fast, smart, funny."
—Kim Stanley Robinson

"Pomo cybertheory never tasted so good!"
—*American Book Review*

"Utterly original."
—Barry N. Malzberg

"If reality is a crutch, Wilson has thrown it away."
—*Rain Taxi*

"A brilliant data screen of future memories."
—Arthur Kroker

"Wilson is both a ghost in the machine and a spanner in the works."
—*The Rumpus*

Battle without Honor or Humanity: Volume 1
Copyright © 2015 by D. Harlan Wilson
ISBN: 978-1-935738-76-3
Library of Congress Control Number: 2015936709

First Paperback Edition, October 2015

All rights reserved. No part of this book may be reproduced, stored in a retrieval system, or transmitted by any means without the written permission of the author and publisher. This is a work of fiction. Published in the United States by Raw Dog Screaming Press.

Acknowledgment is made to the following magazines, journals and anthologies in which some of the stories in this collection originally appeared: *Fiction International, VLAK, The Big Book of Bizarro, Emanations: Second Sight, WTF?!: An Anthology, Black Scat Review, The Dream People, BackLit, Pif Magazine, The Surreal Grotesque* and *Journal of Experimental Fiction*.

Cover Design by Bradley Sharp
www.BradSharp.co.uk

Author Illustration by Goodloe Byron
www.GoodloeByron.tumblr.com

Raw Dog Screaming Press
Bowie, MD

www.RawDogScreaming.com

ALSO BY D. HARLAN WILSON

Biographies
Hitler: The Terminal Biography
Freud: The Penultimate Biography
Douglass: The Lost Autobiography

Novels
Primordial: An Abstraction
The Kyoto Man
Codename Prague
Dr. Identity, or, Farewell to Plaquedemia
Peckinpah: An Ultraviolent Romance
Blankety Blank: A Memoir of Vulgaria

Fiction Collections
Diegeses
They Had Goat Heads

Nonfiction/Criticism
They Live (Cultographies)
Technologized Desire: Selfhood & the Body in Postcapitalist Science Fiction

CONTENTS

Invective • 11
Zapruder • 20
Scotomization • 27
Entelechy • 32
Abattoir • 37
Cognition • 41
Disambiguation • 46
Paraprosdokian • 52
Emissary • 60
Bibliomancer • 65
Autocracy • 72
Directeur • 78
Virulence • 85
Presidency • 91
Battle without Honor or Humanity: Part 1 • 102

For Tomoyasu.

"Dobaded."
—Kawamata Chiaki, *Death Sentences*

Invective

"I have no idea what the word 'criterion' is doing in the first sentence. Now then. What about the intentionality of the speaker, who masquerades as an insurgent Dionysian? This requires much more unpacking and expression. You are a fool, sir, in the best (i.e., Elizabethan) and worst (i.e., *cretin*) senses of the term. I saw you the other night at the burlesque show. You were on stage. You were doing a bad thing—very unclear in its context, and I never use the term 'very' with frivolous intent, especially in light of its utter superfluity in the English language. Something (e.g., the trajectory of your relaxed belligerence) is 'very bad' or simply 'bad'—both usages denote badness. Please don't point the crutch of 'degrees of intensity' at me; bad is bad, 'very' or otherwise. This brings me to a higher echelon of contention. Why is [**name of protagonist**]'s desire 'nuclear' and 'embossed'? These usages, under the aegis of this itinerary, utterly flummox and escape me. In

Invective

addition, you overlook the profound naïveté of [**name of secondary author**]'s analysis of digital reality, which is so obviously about a self-deluded, self-righteous *Pax Americana*. Furthermore, your articulation of a de facto 'messianic oubliette' is symptomatic of a larger problem, namely your unwillingness to engage with the material in any meaningful fashion. Remember when you emceed the Tony Awards? You pretended the ceremonies had nothing to do with music as you gesticulated and spat into the microphone like a dictator whose flock is running away from him even as he bleats. There's more. Careless blunders. Raging embellishments. And does the [**name of subsidiary character**] really exert a 'raw masculinity' and 'defend the ludicrous pomposity of [**bleep**] while looming on the sidelines as two teenagers awkwardly engage in coitus on the hood of a 1967 Chevy Camaro'? We all know that 1967 marks the hairy birth of the Camaro. This is not to undermine the matter at hand: your inviolate slag. Let me assure you that being an academic has its perks. Economy, for instance. By god, I make over two hundred thousand dollars a year to tell young people how much shit they pack between their ears for an hour or so per day; I spend the rest of my time staring out the window and looking at stock quotes while 'writers' whore themselves all over creation just to buy groceries and cigarettes. Bartlebys! But no. Bartleby didn't smoke. He had principles and carried a pocket knife. Well. Most 'writers' lack the discipline to get a Ph.D., let alone hold down a teaching job, or any job—even pumping gas and data entry is too much of a challenge—so who can blame them for their bald degradation? Please stay out of my way when I step over [***Nom du pére***]. Did I mention your galactic capacity? That is because it does not exist. I confess I found the application of terms privileging debates about [**important subjects**] not particularly useful in thinking about a film, a dream, or reality. There is a lot more you could do with the [**title of citation**] raised in the 506th paragraph. Incidentally, if you cook and eat an animal with conjunctivitic eyes—any animal with conjunctivitic eyes—it is likely that you will contract a bona fide terminal disease. Hence: *look to the gaze*. So. I have orders to shoot you on the spot and I've been going on and on like a . . . like a . . . like a what? I don't know. Like somebody who goes on and on. Please stand still. Stand still. I can't aim when you're running back and forth like that. All right, I won't shoot you, but stop it. Thank you." Blam. "I missed. I apologize. I only had one bullet. Now I don't know what to do." Blam. "I missed again. How embarrassing! I had another bullet, but I didn't tell you. You can stand still. I only had two bullets. Really. I'm going to be in Big Trouble on your account. Mind you. Incidentally, your earlier discussion on Queequeg and the denaturalists has massive potential for expansion and development. That's what I always tell my students, no matter what they do: *expand and develop*. They never listen. They do what they want." Blam. "Gotcha! No? Dammit. I guess there was a ghost cartridge in the chamber. Excuse me. I seem to be experiencing a pain in my head. Right here. A very deep and antagonistic pain. I require a narcotic. I'll be right back," said [**name of detractor**].

[**Name of detractor**] stepped outside into the neighborhood, which looked eerie and gray and stolid, like a

Invective

daguerreotype. He ambled into a cul-de-sac and screamed, "Does anybody have a narcotic! I need a narcotic! There's a pain in my head!" He waited for a few minutes until somebody came out and walked into the cul-de-sac and offered him a pill.

"Just one?" said [**name of detractor**].

[**Name of neighbor**] shrugged.

"Do I know you?"

"I'm your neighbor," said [**name of neighbor**]. "I live next door. Right there. The house I just came out of."

[**Name of detractor**] repudiated the narcotic, thanked the neighbor and went back inside.

The sky swallowed a cloud.

[**Name of protagonist**] said, "Long ago I fell in love with a common woman. We indulged in the entire spectrum of human existence in the span of a fortnight. We spoke about everything. We enacted everything. It was a tragedy."

Palsied, [**name of detractor**] replied, "I understand. Have you ever been hurled out of a commercial airliner? My father did that to me once. I wasn't expecting it. I have been mocked before and I will be mocked again. But this business about the 'entire spectrum of human existence' is a red flag. 'Life is nothing more than a sequence of painful separations.' You said that. Those are your words. At any rate, it is my contention that those are your words. You had stormed the entresol of the P'Zhang Theatre. You had jumped onto the railing and were striding up and down it like a funambulist. 'We are born,' you exclaimed, 'and the doctor takes us away from our mother. He tells somebody to give us a bath and then gives us back to our mother, and then we get taken away again, this time by our father, who wants to cuddle with us. There is a lot of back and forth at this point. Later, we are separated from our parents and sent to school. Just when we get used to school, we must go home to our parents. It's confusing. Later, we find a woman who we never want to leave; all day long we lay in bed and fuck like banshees. But we must go to work. And then we have kids together and the cycle begins again. Do you understand?' Something to that effect—that's what you said. On and on you went, soliloquizing with little, if any, original energy. Your thesis was plain enough: there's never enough time to grow roots. And yet you, sir, are an enemy of the root, as your behavior and your discourse, time and again, reify. This is not to say that I don't respect you. Here is my curriculum vitae." [**Name of detractor**] hands a c.v. to [**name of protagonist**]. "As you can plainly see, I have fallen into the proverbial fire pit on multiple occasions; I allowed the flames to consume my flesh, then crawled out of the pit and started again. One must always start again. It is the nature of life. New beginnings. [**Name of God**] would have it no other way." Click. "I swear this gun isn't working." Click. Click. "This piece of shit. It's broken." He moved the barrel from one temple to the other and pulled the trigger again. Click. "I'm going to set the weapon aside. It has ceased to retain a purpose, even as an object of intimidation, even as [**name of the Phallus**]. There. It's done. Do you have any cigars? No? Well. We must celebrate. It's not every day that one fails so excellently to live up to one's potential. If I may. There. Yes. Ahh. My boneless phalanges dangle into the void

Invective

like fulminating counterparts. Are you aware that there is a hole in your [**brand name of jeans**]? Buy some new fucking [**brand name of jeans**]. If you think that I am spying on you, it is very likely that I am spying on you, even as I kneel before you." [**Name of detractor**] kneels. [**Name of detractor**] realizes he is already kneeling. "My irreconcilable vigilance is doubtless the reason I have come down so hard on you this afternoon. Repairing your 'text,' so to speak, may ultimately be a simple matter of linguistic, and hence neurological, fine-tuning. Yes. Yes. Yes. Yes. Yes. Yes. Yes. Yes. Yes. Yes. The egg of the Word came before the chicken of the Brain. No. When you fall into an inverted lotus pose it frightens me; time and again I am reminded of the crabs. More to the point, I acknowledge your intuition, but do you really think you can get away with any kind of intelligent discussion of [**name of discussion subject**] in the absence of an invocation of Ronald Reagan? I don't understand. I . . . Here, let me stand up now. I'm going to stand." He stood. "There. I'm up."

An oubliette of ultraviolence superseded a hardcore sex scene that both [**name of protagonist**] and [**name of detractor**] observed with a calm, detached awareness.

"Tell me something. Will you take a polygraph? No? Fuck you!" exclaimed [**name of detractor**].

Wind blew across the savannah.

"Like I said earlier," continued [**name of detractor**], "You should retain no hard feelings for me. I didn't say that? Well, I'm saying it now. I am not cruel or antagonistic by nature, but if you fuck me, I will fuck you back twice as hard. Apologies in advance. The fact is people need other people to tell them what they're doing wrong. Otherwise we are little more than antelopes wandering up and down the streets of Pangea, alone, ornery, drunk on cactus water and riddled by existential dread. Have you ever attended the Human Trafficking Convention? No? They teach you how to exploit human beings with flair and panache. I have been to every convention. I have attended all of the conventions, everywhere, on everything and everyone. I don't often pay attention to the panelists and the lecturers, even when I am serving on a panel or presenting a lecture, preferring instead to scrutinize the audience and take attendance. Let me tell you who attended my funeral. [**Litany of names**]. Do you hear that? Just to be sure. [**Litany of names.**]" In the distance, monkeys screeched, elephants trumpeted. "What can I say? The jungle follows me everywhere I go. As for the yawning chasm of your existence, well, I wish you all the very best. I am going to step in that [**name of hole**] over there now." He steps in the [**name of hole**]. From the bottom, he says, "I'm in the [**name of hole**] now! Don't forget about me! The worst thing somebody can do to you is forget about you! Are you still there! Is anybody there! I'm all by myself down here! Help! Help!"

[**Name of protagonist**] helped [**name of detractor**] out of [**name of hole**]. There was nothing left to say.

"Thank you very much," said [**name of detractor**]. "Let me add that I don't like it when handmaidens perform sexual rites on the stage of Forever. Spin it any way you please: I just don't like it, and I never will. You mention something to this

Invective

effect in your sixty-third zeitgeist. Immediately thereafter you entertain the subject of gerontology. I do not understand the smell of elderly human beings. They all emit the same pong. They walk by me and the pong nearly knocks me off of my stilts. I think there is some kind of secret at work here to which I am less than privy. You reach a certain age and you become part of this club. The price: wear this perfume and traumatize a considerable percentile of the Human Stain. The younger percentile. The fact of the matter is that I am quite old and nobody has approached me about said club or said troublesome perfume. Speaking of which, why do you keep mentioning Humbert Humbert in a so-called 'slack-jawed manifesto' that has nothing at all to do with the wayward desires of a certain dirty old man? I could go on. And I will. There was a time when stiltwalkers existed under the thumb of a kind of anti-stiltwalking regime. 'Punish stiltwalkers,' was their mantra. Again I failed to experience any sort of involvement with the oppressed demographic, as if I had always-already been standing on my own two feet. I suppose you look at me and you see a man doing just that, standing here in absentia the fabled apparatuses." [**Name of detractor**] looked down and regarded himself sadly. "Indeed. There they are. The lack of the apparatuses."

"There they are. The lack of the apparatuses," echoed [**name of protagonist**].

"Do you ever get the feeling that your molecules are dirty?" rejoined [**name of detractor**]. "I experience this feeling at least twice a day. My molecules feel like Biblical whores—the filth beneath the fingernails of Filth. Again, I convey these sentiments with the greatest of intentions.

BATTLE WITHOUT HONOR OR HUMANITY

Viz., I intend to help you 'improve.' What's that you say? What? What? What? What? What? What? What? What? Say again? I'm not entirely sure I heard what you said."

"There they are. The lack of the apparatuses," echoed **[name of protagonist]**.

There was nothing left to say.

Wind blew across the savannah.

The sky swallowed a cloud.

"Just one?" said **[name of detractor]**.

Blam.

Now then.

"I have no idea what the expression 'syncopated' is doing in the second to the last sentence. Nonetheless I hope these thoughts are of use to the author in revising his gestalt for publication since it does contain a lot of not-yet-fulfilled promise."

Zapruder

I grow out of SpectraVision. Or I grow into it. Whatever the case, I achieve an impressive basal metabolism . . .

Confused, I retain an 8mm zoomatic camera and shoot footage of a murder in progress.

It's happening in the bathroom.

The door creaks open. I move closer. An expanding sliver of light reaches across the carpet like a dead Fury.

I adjust the dual electric eye of the camera. The marginalized selenium cell compensates for any paraxial backlight.

I kick in the door and manipulate the button on the roof of the turret, converging on the subject matter . . .

A gunman shoots a prostitute who has curled into the bow of a deep tub.

The gun is loud and doesn't make a sound. Nor does it fire bullets.

Every time the gunman pulls the trigger, an exploding hole forms in the prostitute's flesh, spraying the tile with arrases of blood and booze. The pastels instigate an idle hermeneutic. And yet she seems to wax the pain without effort or beguilement.

It occurs to me that the prostitute may be a prominent local senator.

He screams and never dies.

Nonplussed, I run out of tape and reload the camera with another magazine.

Nothing fazes the gunman. He shoots the senator until he catches a glimpse of himself in the mirror and then we go outside in the backyard where a situationist has cuckolded an elderly matron.

Feeling safe, he sets the gun aside and places a conch against his ear.

Sound of *arche-écriture* . . .

In the absence of weapons and artillery, death scenes experience a calm and quiet eviction. Causality tightens into a crooked fist. This instant marks the beginning of a serious *mode de vie*. What appears to have been a sequence of schizophrenic, absurdist, whimsical *passages des actes* congeals into a linear and no-nonsense scenario. I shoot the material with a curiosity that fondles the dirt. Nothing really happens. I listen to the camera's spring-wound mechanism, the synthesis of hums and purrs and clicks and clacks.

My gaze unfolds into an accordion of celluloid.

By force of will, I zoom in on an ex post facto hostage situation. The victims have been disemboweled by an indolent executioner who didn't once finish the job. Thereafter he cauterized the stomach wounds and hung them, one at a time, behind the Sixth Wall, wrists pinned to their ankles with massive iron staples.

Zapruder

One of the hostages recognizes my vigilance. I zoom into her eye.

The cornea glistens and trembles and tells a story. Each chapter concludes with a powerful, calculated blink, and the eyelids fall together like aluminum curtains.

I zoom out just in time to capture this blooper: a troupe of Ottoman soldiers march into Constantinople and openfire on an abandoned Hippodrome, exhuming a Byzantine empire from the graveyard of permanence.

A chancellor penetrates the diegesis and attempts to usurp the authority of a Benedictine monk. He underestimates his opponent's rank and devolves into clarity.

"One day," intones the monk, "I will punish all of the interpellators."

Giving me the hairy eyeball, he wants to say more, and he needs to: the assertion, as it stands, lacks context and ultimately meaning and purpose. I don't see any interpellators, after all.

The monk remains silent. Devout.

I bring him in and out of focus, calling his contours into question. The meter sensors at the bottom of the screen flare and whirl like slot machines.

I continue to shoot footage.

The streets of Cannes reek with the midnight piss of glitterati, starfuckers and drama whores, but I follow the rules and make the scene, recording the evaporation of dewdrops from the hood of a futuristic omnibus parked outside La Chunge, a piano bar and restaurant depressurized by 1950s Parisian décor and nonrefundable set pieces. I got drunk there last night with Victor Bleep and

BATTLE WITHOUT HONOR OR HUMANITY

Monica Seles. Respective celebrities of eternity and yore. At the conclusion of every martini, the retired tennis player solemnly lifted her blouse and showed me the knife wound. "Nobody remembers my talent on the court," she slurred. "Only the gash in my flank."

The memory explodes across my mindscape like a ring of atomic fire ... and I feel the sun on my bald spot.

I have forgotten to put on lotion.

There's no time. The submission deadline expires in minutes and I still have to edit the film.

I study the reel for hours and take refuge on a deserted veranda that overlooks the bay. Every piece of upturned furniture reeks of abandonment and lacklove. I might be forty stories skyward.

I sit on the ledge and shoot the veranda even though the camera isn't loaded anymore.

Somehow I harvest a recording and thread it into the rest of the footage. It is this new ghost footage that distinguishes my film as a bona fide work of danger and recognition. Critics sense its existence immediately and reviews decant from the aqueducts like so much cheap hooch.

I thread the reviews into the footage and produce an even stronger picture that itself produces more reviews and revises the Critical Psyche. The process of splicing and reproduction invokes the promise of eternity but eventually you have to make a choice.

I contract a hitman to take out a critic—just one critic— and divert attention from my Primary Text.

The subsequent investigation timelapses across the crime scene as detectives and police officers and forensics experts gather information and finger an innocent man. By then I have already showered, shaved, and rented a stretch limo . . .

I exit the limo and stand on the gray carpet that leads into the showroom.

Nobody takes my picture.

An usher pulls me by the wrist to a seat in the mezzanine, stroking my elbow with a careful thumb.

The lights are off.

I smell mothballs and liquor and analgesic cream.

Across the amphitheater a sign I can't read glints like the North Star.

The lights flicker on.

The orchestra pit bears a likeness to a meteor crater. Nothing remains but the scorched earth.

The gunman appears onstage.

He has aged by at least fifty years and makes the following announcement to the audience in a slow, controlled, posh-Russian falsetto: "Good evening. I am an old man. I am a sick man . . ."

The microphone squelches out and nobody can hear the rest of his speech.

It come backs on as he introduces the film . . . "which is a feat of venerable egoism in light of the apparatus the auteur used to manufacture this belligerent *objet d'art*. I've a mind to gun down the fucker. But I gave that up years ago in favor of more philanthropic pursuits." He pauses and shoots the A-list hookers in the front row, all of whom squawk like dignitaries and prefects at the helm. "In good cinema, the end always brings us back to the beginning in interesting ways. That's why this film succeeds. There is no *logique circulaire*. The text fires into the sky like a hellnote and scalds the cosmos. *Fin*. This is the way it must be done."

A trap door opens beneath the gunman, swallows him, and spits him out. He lands on his feet as if nothing happened, then hobbles offstage.

The opening credits fade into intelligibility.

They are all Names of the Father.

Noms des Peres.

Hallowed, I get bored and walk offscreen.

This is the part of the show where mere corrosion eclipses the windup bird of extinction.

Here is a mnemonic Polaroid of late twenty-first century Dallas, Texas, chronicled from the bowels of a highly subjectivized outrézone.

In the distance, Bavarian saloons dot the snowcapped mountaintops and remind us of hypermediatized acne.

Closer, mirrored gondolas mark the key coordinates on a lattice of wires in the sky.

Cloudstains melt on the tarmac.

Emaciated buttes rise from the dust into the icecold atmosphere.

And in the dust, the aftermath of an ultraviolent gunfight showcases entire tapestries of logical, indexical exenteration, of brains and skullpieces draped across the Black Trunk.

The Trunk is all that matters.

And the Ideologues.

And wine.

Zapruder

I remember the past like it was yesterday. I glide above the ramparts in a rickety commuter jet and the long corridor induces claustrophobia, anxiety, dread, acceptance. I see an ape on the beach. In my dreams, the beach always foregrounds the solitude of an ape.

I remember nothing else beyond the appetites of palsied smiles and burning circuitry.

Scotomization

To form a mental blind spot...

I had been part of the Kennedys' inner circle for so long I could barely remember the finer details of my indoctrination, with the exception of the hazing ceremony, during which I was ordered to stand naked in the library of the Aquinnah Estate and hold a hot tamale between my teeth as the Kennedys shouted obscenities and laughed at my anthropomorphic shortcomings. Whenever my lips faltered and grazed the tamale, they burst aflame...

Daylight.

Noon.

Enemies fired from the surf of the Incurable Coast—heat missiles carved a black frown in the sky. We had to usher the Kennedys across the ocean. I dressed in an adrenalized fury, opting for a clip-on tie. The lady of the manor pleaded with me to don the Real Thing and presented to me her upturned diorama on a hand-painted

Scotomization

Victorian platter. I reluctantly turned her down. I knew I would regret it. But there was no time.

Jack and Lee were in the guesthouse rolling and smoking cigarettes. The place smelled like barcodes; they had just skinned a llama and draped the hide over a chaise to dry. The underparts of the animal had been dissected and primed for the proverbial All Out Praxis. Nobody in the family wasted anything. "The sky is frowning like a Irishman," I reminded them. "We need to get underwater."

Lee salvaged whatever accruals of tobacco could be stuffed into a shirt and he and Jack shoved their arms into powerful frock coats that seemed to move of their own volition. I ushered them outside, the stigma indelible as mushroom clouds leapt onto the horizon like bullfrogs. Already the vines had begun to shrivel. Soon the plasma would turn to rust.

"Mind the guardrail," said Betty as we fell into the chute and stepped aboard a submarine.

The roots of Martha's Vineyard hung in the water like withered udders . . . I placed my hand against the glass wall of the aquarium. Warm to the touch. The air was thick and infinitely green . . . The captain tripped and fell into the control panel. Sparks leapt from unmanned wires and he caught fire. Eddie tackled the captain with a horse blanket, put out the flames and accidentally suffocated him.

There was a ceremony on the fly bridge and the Kennedys threw a collective fit. I respected the upheaval, eyes fixed on clasped hands. If the mutiny occurred before the ship set sail, technically there could be no mutiny.

BATTLE WITHOUT HONOR OR HUMANITY

A fruitfly landed on my arm. I killed it.

Anatomy of a submarine: conning tower, sleeping quarters, boiler room, trim and ballast tanks, nuclear reactor, ballistic missile repository, Cold War wine cellar, snorkel, anechoic plating...

Perception as a red hatchet.

Fidel wanted to drive. He had put on the captain's frayed, smoldering hat to ensure that nobody argued with him. Nikolai punched him. Fidel punched him back. They clutched one another by the lapels of their suits and threw one another from side to side and then they crashed through a decayed floor panel and fell out of sight. Jackie salvaged the hat and slipped behind the helm... Octopi and squid covered the nose of the sub. She shook them off, violently, yanking on the controls. Her forearm inflated with color and I traced the cephalic vein from wrist to crook with my fingernail...

...predetermined saboteur. The impromptu dialogue quickly evolved into another ceremony imbricating all of the major players. Accusations and accidental blowups produced corresponding plyboard-partitioned tristes. Procedural disputes coiled into jurisdictional wranglings. I tripped over the rhetorical morass like a wounded calf. Eventually I paid for it. The catalyst, claimed Bobby: my Gaelic upper lip—"interminably long and menacing."

Dry land.

Rancorous indictments.

Infernal Affairs briskly took me aside and chastised me. They unplugged the Zapruder camera in the interrogation room and pushed me into a chair by the shoulders. "Why

Scotomization

don't you like me," was Teddy's opening line. "I like you. I like everyone who breathes the Rich Substance."

I said, "I don't know why I don't like you. I think it has something to do with that shiteating grin etched into your puss." The grin folded together like curtains. I shrugged. "I've got nothing to say."

"All right," said Teddy. "You can go then."

I got up to leave.

"Sit the fuck down asshole!"

The others looked on as Teddy sat across the table from me and tilted his head. "I have to speak to you immediately," he said. He stood and exited the room. Eddie came in and said he was serving as Assistant to the District Attorney in Joey's absence. A waiter served zweibacks from a misshapen porcelain plate that threatened to topple off of his palm. We observed a luminescent battle grid. Blips raced up and down the fractal lines. Eddie took me by the shirt and said, "I'm trying to communicate with you. This is a *communiqué*. What's wrong with you?"

"Nothing. I'm just a glacier monkey like everybody and their mother."

I kept talking until somebody acquiesced, expressing interest in my belief system. It was John, Jr. Once I had him on my side everybody else fell into rank. I received a formal letter of apology and forgiveness at a ceremony presided over by a Kennedy without a Name (KwN). We drank a lot of brandy and then the family doctor performed mock electroshock therapy on me, easing me onto a rollaway bed, placing a leather bit in my mouth, and producing a series of wet alveopalatal shocking sounds.

BATTLE WITHOUT HONOR OR HUMANITY

Marilyn wheeled me up to the honeymoon suite.

Somebody turned out the lights.

I awoke in the early morning. John was sitting on the end of the bed in his favorite gray suit, elbows on knees, swishing the last drops of scotch in the basin of a rocks glass. The shoulder-to-shoulder articulation of his back preoccupied me.

I sat up in bed and the covers fell into my lap.

"I don't like crowds, is the thing," noted John in his signature accent. "I have social anxiety. But nobody will prescribe me medication. That's why I drink so much. And the drinking makes me talk funny. I don't know what to do." He reached behind him and laid a hand on Marilyn's exposed ankle. She didn't wake up. I suspected she might have passed away in her sleep.

The last thing I remembered was the smell of coffee, the sound of the percolator. The angled silhouette of a man set against a tall bay window.

Entelechy

Dawn. When the bandwidth incites primacy. And a glib culpability. I discover the hangmen performing certain rites of passage. They call these rites "liquid furies."

In blank facemasks with eyeholes slashed into the fabric, the hangmen slip orbitoclasts into thawed and bristled icemen, one at a time. Nascent agony rises from the pyre. Here is the pecuniary element of the Reich. They attach electroshock cables to the icemen's dominant extremities. A span of time elapses prior to general administration during which the hangmen confer in excited whispers. Pulse-currents flow from an ECT machine into the victims. Eyes and nostrils and mouths aglow, their chests come apart like unclasped fingers, exposing no ribcage, no lungs or heart, but a constellation of unhinged macaque heads, with faces shaved and painted white, the kernels of Aztec warriors. All of the iceman reveal the same interior of anxiety . . .

BATTLE WITHOUT HONOR OR HUMANITY

I go to a familiar café and ask to be seated on the east veranda. Everything is as it should be. Nobody remembers me, and there's no veranda, and they don't serve lunch until the fascia of the moon appears in the sky at a critical distance from the sun.

Balkan diagnostics confiscate the mise en scène.

I order a Turkish coffee and sit at a table next to the window. The coffee tastes like Absence, but I force it down, swallowing in pained fits of strangulation, confident that, in time, my palate will either acclimatize to the taste or become immune to it. Outside the window, the Leaning Tower of Pisa angles away from its host cathedral, dipping to the grass like a drinking bird and then snapping back into the sky. Tourists shoot footage with outdated photographic and filmmaking equipment. Occasionally their attention wanders and the tower smashes them when it goes down.

I had not been to Pisa for years. I'm not there now.

I remember the tower's Aggression. I remember the winding streets, the bridges over the Arno, the façade of Santa Maria della Spina, the isosceles men who appeared beside me whenever I experienced congestion or stomach cramps. As expected, the last thing I remember about Pisa is impetuously geometric, the way the contours of reality folded into a central asterisk, limning new realms of sensoria.

It's getting late. I awake in a vast display case. Halogen lights. Wooden panelling on the walls and ceiling and floor. Smells like ammonia. Ripples of boiled celluloid retreat to the perimeter... The mannequins encircle me. I don't know them. Striking poses of intense confidence or dangerous whimsicality, the males wear tertiary, sharp-shouldered dinner suits, the females morbid lingerie. I have been shrinkwrapped with a dense polymer, tightly, bound like a fly in a spiderweb, although I can still manipulate my arms and legs.

Somebody smashes the display case with a crowbar, leaps in and attacks me without attitude. His face has been painted shoepolish black, like a vervet. It might be a latex mask. It might belong to a thoroughbred simian. He swings the crowbar at me and I awkwardly duck out of the way and he hits a mannequin and the mannequin explodes into tasteless flecks of porcelain . . . Fatigued and deranged, my attacker balks. I'm able to wrestle the crowbar away from him and club him over the head. I continue to club him until all semblance of a face, human or otherwise, disappears. "I'm done," I announce.

I fall out of the display case, conscious of an audience, but unwilling to ascribe to myself even the most primitive of dissembling airs. I start running, limbs stiff, as if my knees and elbows have been soldered together. I try to tear the shrinkwrap off as I go.

I can't do two things at once.

Run or tear.

I stop to make a decision. There is no decision.

It's dark now. I don't recall what a solar anus looks like. I fail to understand the authority of a corona.

In the corner, an old projector flings images of grey forests onto a wall. Dissonant bustle of foliage. A man charges onscreen. Plain. Effete. He strokes the elongated shaft of a wireless microphone, then buries it in the leaves, the roots . . . He observes me closely, eyes describing an epistemology of horror.

Sobriety weakens me like a fever. I escape down a Grecian hallway that terminates in a forgotten attic. Something bad happened here, I know, but the evidence is circumstantial and exists only in the form of a mental effigy. And yet circumstantial evidence has produced guilty verdicts. This insight obscures all notions of growth and subversion.

The attic is empty and clean and outfitted with faux wood panels. Light shines through a small octagonal window on the far end. The floorboards creak as I step towards it.

A figure so thin he lacks identifiable features steps out of a shadow and wards me off.

I stop. "What's out there?"

He shakes the withered conch of his head.

I move forward, lean over, and peer out the window.

Entelechy informs my delirium vis-à-vis the revision of a mudpenny. My ego surges like the cosmos. I still can't process what I see . . . until I see it clearly.

The yard is familiar and yet I have never seen it before. Dead grass stretches over an acre to a tall wrought-iron gate. Nothing beyond it. There are dead oak trees with gnarled branches, long holes that might be exhumed graves, and bushes in flames. The sky is too blue and too clean and too alive.

I touch the window. Pixels smear.

I look over my shoulder. The window falls off.

Entelechy

Shatters.

Liquid furies roll between my toes like ocean surf. Then my knees, my hands . . . I accomplish a slow crawl with no identifiable destination, pulling something behind me. It slants out of my abdomen and etches a cruel trajectory in the sand . . . a catheter . . . a jellyfish . . . I feel my insides collapse into an avid scream. I need to obtain the retroactive channel, the source of the hangmen's mania and imagination. The process may result in readymade hieroglyphics that bear their wounds to the eyes of renunciation. It keeps coming . . . and I keep going, decayed and banished by my own orgones . . . I lay my head in the broth. I breathe in the suds of countless enemies and worry about how I will experience the morning. The morning can be cruel but the morning can be therapeutic, even liberating, although never histrionic.

Unresponsive, I come to rest on the infinite plateau of a sundial, awaiting the turn of shadows.

Abattoir

Courtesy reminder: ... handle the inscribed *esprit de finesse* with extreme care. Failure to pollute the waters of Irk with your corporeal referendum may incite mortal, oozing skin rashes. This is not an acid test. The university reputation survey applies to everyone that falls into the aforementioned demographic and must be processed and completed in a timely fashion. Mind the office partitions on your way to the gas chamber. Inhale the content. Die.

Sound of a cue ball striking a fresh rack ...

A prison guard drags me down the corridor by an iron ankle bracelet that repeatedly twists and cracks the bones as we turn corners. They have removed the meatslab from my head, but my sensorium still works, and I scream like a slaughtered calf.

In place of the brain: a minute receptor that hangs in the vacuum of my empty skull, glinting like a distant star. The bog itself lacks a dreamlife in spite of rabid sentience.

Abattoir

I don't know why this is the case. I suspect some manner of scientific curiosity or plaintive sadism, both of which generate the same effects. But I see everything as if my facilities remain intact.

Enter the ludic element of this precession. The visage of the noir antihero oscillates between detailed estuaries of expression and deliberate iconic abstraction. In the Quotidian tradition, a pedagogy of valence marks the soft coordinates. I behead minotaurs and outplay mariachis—nothing escapes my amniotic jaws. Moral and social disillusionment is as inexorable as static cling.

I have been incarcerated for bad acting. The gender performativity with which I unfold and flaunt my extremities and membranes has received only lukewarm acclaim. They don't know what to do with me. The illusion of internment will suffice for now. And so I move forward as I look backward. Meanwhile a fresh, arbitrary rant interrupts the weather report:

"Please turn to page 36 in our textbook. I want to talk about my molecules. I want to talk about my molecules. I want to talk about my molecules. I want to talk about my molecules. I want to talk about my molecules. I want to talk about my molecules. I want to talk about my molecules. I want to talk about my molecules. I want to talk about my molecules. I want to talk about my molecules. Not to discount the primacy of my individual atoms."

At this crucial moment in my quest for Being Left Alone, I develop a penchant for tear gas. I always carry seven or eight marbles of the chemical compound in the pockets of my trousers, fingering them like spare change. Whenever a complicated social equation presents itself—an awkward conversation, a disagreement with a mechanic about the price of car repair, an idle distaste for the tone with which somebody addresses me—in short, anything that spikes my blood pressure—I nonchalantly slip on a pair of gas goggles, hold my breath, and slam a marble onto the earth between me and my oppressor. Corneal nerves flail like severed worms. Of course, I laced the gas with a powerful insecticide, if only to teach myself a lesson that I never seem to learn: ALWAYS MONITOR AND MANAGE YOUR EXPECTATIONS . . .

The pulsar in my noosphere informs me that my exhumed brain has attempted to bully a watchman from the incubation beaker in which it floats. Immersed in proverbial subarachnoid fluid, the brain bobs up and down like a mutant bar of soap and attacks the watchman with invisible "heat-rays." I have neither prompted nor encouraged this corny scientific romance. Sometimes cognition carves its own groove into the Woodblock.

The floor escapes me . . . We have entered the Blood Cell. The prison guard hangs me upside down by the same ankle that has already been mangled. More bones break, cracking like popcorn in boiling oil. As the foot slowly separates from the leg, the guard intones, "I don't like ugly people. I don't mean figuratively. I don't mean 'ugly on the inside.' I mean people who are ugly. They offend me. I don't like them." Shrieking now, I recognize that he is a handsome man.

And we recognize the inevitability of what we have known all along: the fate of my extremity annoys me as

Abattoir

much as the smell of dry leaves and the devolved memories that leap to attention like evicted pogo sticks. An askance look rankles me like a death blow. This happens all the time. This is consciousness.

I represent adventure and carnage. I perform endless Shakespearean soliloquies, nailing every syllable to the drywall, and fling myself into the mosh pit, where painted flowerchildren mark me for a killer. Then I am in the desert. A sentinel confiscates my passport and revises the core information. Acid rain has carved deep, thin grottos in the sand.

I move over the topography with ghostwhite steps.

Cognition

I drew closer to the object-cause of my desire, my face an ageless mask of concentration, like a Sphinx. It was the same expression I had worn when I fell off the mountain. An accidental hang glider took a photograph with a telescopic camera and gave it to me later that day, after I had been released from the test site and thoroughly debriefed and disambiguated. I studied the photograph. There I was, falling, head forced upwards by the hard wind, awkwardly, like a marionette puppet with a snapped neck. The mouth on the puppet was a listless slot and it regarded the hang glider with wooden eyes that suggested something between wild indifference and purposeful obligation. I don't remember how it felt. Surely I worried about dying an explosive death, but I had no recollection of emotion, and while I did "explode" against the earth, so to speak, I failed to break any bones, let alone die. I was back on my feet before I realized I was off them.

Cognition

Scarlet vestiges of dusk threaded into midnight.

Two basic emotions constitute the human sensorium: FEAR, and the ABSENCE OF FEAR. In simpler terms: plus and minus, possession and lack. Everything else is a vindictive subcategory.

I can never seem to resolve which end of the spectrum commands my feelings. The answer is always LACK. But sometimes the realm of surfaces comes to bear. And the realm of surfaces always functions as a metaphysical trump card.

Children stand on the curb and produce echolalia.

A patrol car pulls over and idles at the curbside for at least two minutes with the sirens blasting. The windows are tinted but you can see silhouettes moving around inside.

Gradually the sirens get slower and quieter, scaring the children, until all you can hear is a drunken slur.

Then silence.

The door swings open.

As the driver steps out, the airbag explodes out of the steering wheel, crystalizing his aviator sunglasses and pinning him against the doorjamb. It is as if the airbag had been waiting for him to turn his back on it. He struggles with the airbag. The children watch. He can't get free. Or get out. Or get away. He punches the airbag and drops elbows on the airbag and screams at the airbag but nothing works. It's a strong airbag. Finally he squeezes his hand between his stomach and the airbag and sort of inches down his torso with his fingers until he gets a good grip on the handle of the hunting knife in his utility belt. Fascinated, the children trade anxious whispers. The driver yanks the knife out, severing the airbag like a stag's bladder. The children cheer as the driver is tarred-and-feathered by the airbag's contents—a mix of cornstarch, chalkdust and talcum powder ignited by nitrogen gas—but when the airbag deflates and its raw material relaxes into the front seat, the children's excitement quickly threads into Arboreal Dread, a liminal crisis that one day consumes us all, piecemeal at first, and then full-throttle into the Brown Gorge.

This could be happening in a different story. See the end of "Paraprosdokian," the narrative of which happens concurrently.

But that story is another story and flirts with cinematic hokum. The connectivity. There may be none. Accuracy falls to the wayside every time. We can only try to pin Accuracy against a corkboard like a butterfly that refuses to die, flapping its tigerlily wings like an evil elfen banshee.

This is the real story.

Last night at an upscale motel I played Texas Holdem with the sharks and lost $20k in two hours. We were in the courtyard. I kept going to the money machine across the street. I don't remember much. I won one round. I took too much Xanax. I drank a pint of Southern Comfort. I felt good. Happy. When I passed out, the sharks stole my wallet and left me in a bush. When the first rays of the morning sun shone on my face, I awoke as if electrocuted. I went to my room and took a shower. The cheap lemon-scented soap made me dry-heave. I called my wife and told her about the money. I realized I wasn't married and dialed a new number.

"Hello?" I said. "Hello? Hello? Hello? Hello?"

"I'm here," said a voice.

My subsequent confession dovetailed into a vortex of Truth. "Sometimes all that is needed is a sentence," I began. "One sentence and everything falls into place. By which I mean one thought, one act of cognition. I refer to the neural pathways, of course. Always. There is no difference between 'syntax,' per se, and 'genitals,' as it were. I could go on and on about the subject. And I will. Let me tell you about the shirt I was wearing on the morning of my death. I jumped off of a bridge and left a suicide note in the back seat of my Prius. The note was quite short and when I was done composing it I decided to initial it rather than write out my entire signature from start to finish, which would have taken a lot longer. The note read:

THE FOLLOWING DEATH HAS BEEN APPROVED FOR RESTRICTED AUDIENCES ONLY BY THE MOTION PICTURE ASSOCIATION OF AMERIKA

Then, in the lower right-hand corner of the note, I inscribed my initials, like I said, circled three times over for added effect. But I've already gotten away from the shirt. It's not entirely important. As with all of my shirts, the collar was a giant, sharp, raging thing—more like a paisley bat stretching its wings than a collar. Then there were the buttons and the sleeves and so forth. It was just a shirt, really. Honestly. Don't listen to me like that. I can hear you listening. Your silence seems to suggest that in some way my shirt, the presence of my shirt, its existential aggression, functioned as a legitimate rape of the entire fashion world. I can assure you that 'legitimate rape' is a concept that only exists in the minds of old men with weird lips and bony foreheads. In other words, there is no such thing as 'legitimate rape.' And yet I continue to repeat the term. Legitimate rape. Legitimate rape. Is it true that if you say something long enough that it comes true? If nothing else, we must attend to repetition at every turn; the recurrence of a word or phrase points directly at our discourse as much as our body parts."

"Legitimate rape," said the voice.

Offended, I hung up.

Which brings us back to the present moment. Even though we claw for the future in an attempt to escape the past, there is no denying the present moment. As you know by now, I have foregrounded the present moment on several occasions throughout the course of this whorling secretion. Its missive is palpable, practical.

The children stare into the Brown Gorge. In the blue distance, a hang glider drowsily circles a Swiss alp.

The children do not see it.

Disambiguation

At the gym, a man invites me to his wedding. He has spotted me several times on the bench press, encouraging me to push harder in a squawking basso, as if he were the one beneath the bar. Otherwise we have no relationship. I might not recognize him if I passed him on the street. I assume he has few, if any, friends and family and accept the offer with a counterfeit laugh.

Enjoying a post-workout pump, especially in my biceps and thighs, I collect a suit at the cleaners and purchase a new tie. The wedding is tomorrow morning, at 6 a.m., north of the meridian. I call my wife and tell her about the event. "I don't know if I'm allowed to bring a date," I say. "I assume I am. But can I make that assumption? Can I assume anything?"

I can't remember the groom's name. It occurs to me I never knew it. I describe him to my wife and she says she knows him; last week, he leaned in and stole a kiss as she performed mindful leg extensions. "I didn't see him coming," she admits. "I pay careful attention to form and the process of breathing. Sometimes I get lost in my head."

"Head," I echo.

She huffs, offended either by my response or the incident. "His mustache is crooked and it tickled my overlip," she goes on. "You'd think he'd make it straight. Well, that's what happened."

After some discussion, I decide it's best to attend the wedding alone and tell my wife I won't be home for breakfast. I never eat breakfast anyway.

A stretch limousine picks me up at the corner store. Inside the groomsmen await me like friendly attack dogs. They wear casual but fashionable tuxedos with supersharp shoulders and black Chuck Taylors. The groom's absence concerns me. So does everybody's reticence to talk about or even mention it.

Most of the groomsmen are in good spirits and relatively sober. They talk among themselves quietly and politely while sipping chilled spritzers. One groomsman sleeps like a corpse, open mouth sunk into a waterlogged cheek. His chest isn't moving. Small blue pills litter his jacket and I worry that he may be, in fact, dead. Another groomsman hands me a spritzer and says, "There's fish oil in that. Your heart will thank you for the Omega-3s." As I take the drink, the sleeping groomsman, slouched in his seat, wakes long enough to select a pill from his lapel and swallow it. He selects another pill and bites it in half, then looks at me with trembling eyes and nods off again.

Disambiguation

The limo driver takes us to the reception and we remind him about the wedding. He rolls down the divider and there is a long discussion about directions and semantics during which two groomsmen covertly exit the limo, storm a gazebo and confiscate several varieties of appetizers, explaining to the staff that they have been sent on orders from the father-of-the-bride to see that the reception is being set up properly and that the food doesn't taste like shit. They return to the limo and spread the wealth. The driver puts up the divider and we go downtown to the Masonic Temple. He parks in front and helps us out, offering his hand to each groomsman. I marvel at the architecture as he escorts us into the church.

"What religion is the groom?" I ask a greeter. "Is this a mosque? This doesn't look like a mosque."

The greeter regards me as if I have cursed aloud in a children's museum. "Archdiocese," he says begrudgingly.

"Archdiocese?" I look at my hands. "What is that? A person?"

The interior of the temple looks like a hollowed-out whale. An involuted ribcage of stairways envelops the vast, sloping walls . . . Baptismal workstations have been situated beneath colossal stained glass windows; meek-looking priests operate the consoles and await wedding-goers who need a quick fix. One of them signals me. Sweat stains expand across his tunic from the neck, armpits and navel. I acknowledge his attention and turn with a quick jerk . . .

A large woman wearing Old Person perfume hugs me. "It's so nice to see you again!" she bleats. I've never seen her before. She pushes me aside and hugs the next groomsman and says the same thing to him. He nods at me from the cushion of her shoulder. The large woman whispers loudly into his ear: "I took 10 mg of melatonin last night. The dreams I had! You were in all of them." She moved on to another groomsman...

Nearby, somebody says, "If you drive a train fast enough, it will start to howl and moan like a pig on the spit. I've done it. I've heard it."

Still no sign of the groom.

I mingle halfheartedly with the rest of the wedding party and the bride's extended family. A distant uncle tells me not to invest in NASDAQ stocks. A twice-removed cousin tells me she smells desperation on my breath. I flirt with the mother-of-the-bride's headmistress outside the coatroom in the narthex.

I need a cigarette.

I quit smoking a long time ago but occasionally social situations exhume the need. I go outside and nobody's smoking. I ask around and nobody smokes. Frustration. Panic. Then the craving evaporates and I feel refreshed.

An accordion player begins his first set.

Accidental members of the wedding party duck aside to be baptized. The priests only give out towels for sizeable donations. Nobody presents an offering. Holy water drips onto shoulders, collars and cleavagelines.

A marriage counselor announces his presence with a sharp whistle. He tells a flat joke with a dirty punch line. Silence. Distressed, he initiates the wedding rehearsal, going through blocking techniques and explaining acceptable modalities of expression. Thereafter he signals the

Disambiguation

accordion player and an agonized rendition of Canon in D escapes the squeezebox. The groom doesn't show up for either event and I am asked to stand in for him. I know any sign of apprehension of my part will lead to surefire hostility, so I accept the role without a struggle, and I kiss the bride and suck on her neck and ears . . .

In the limo, we eat shrimp scampi and drink a pinot grigio that effectively compliments the flavors of the meat. The groomsman with the pills on his chest continues in the vein of catatonic sleep. Only a few pills remain and his mouth has fallen into an inhuman geometry.

The groom appears at the reception. He has been there all along, "getting drunk and doing pushups," he tells me, bellowing . . . Tall and angular, he wears a beige seersucker suit to "counter hyperhydrosis. The slightest beam of light makes me sweat. In this suit, though, I feel as if I can conquer the sun." His mouth dies like a stain.

During dinner, the groom paws his wife and pinches cocktail waitresses. Elderly couples eyeball one another with archaic disdain. The best man sits to the right of the bride and drinks too much coffee. Instead of making him jittery, it depresses him, physically and emotionally. He can't explain the effect. It has never happened before. He can barely stand to give his speech, he feels so badly, but he finds the energy, and he says, "Heaven swarms with monsters. With a tall enough ladder, I can climb there." He falls back into his chair and stares at the chickenfat on his plate.

Tentative applause.

I excuse myself.

BATTLE WITHOUT HONOR OR HUMANITY

I wander around the reception hall, looking for the bathroom. Balanced psalms and tangled metamorphoses unfold across long, panoramic paintings on the walls—I observe the narrative idly at first, looking awry, then lose myself in the intricate depths of the plot.

I meet somebody. Eyebrows like a widening gyre. Good vascularity. "I have a paper cut," he says, showing me. "Could you tell me where I might find a stereo?"

I point him in the right direction. Indifferent, he issues me a stationary gesture.

"It's my birthday today," I tell him.

"How old are you?"

"Forty."

"Forty? Halfway home."

"I will never see eighty," I remark.

"Halfway home," he says. "Halfway home. Halfway home..."

On the roadside, I contemplate the fibrillations of my heart. Nothing consoles me like temperance. I signal the vanguard, as if frightened, and I imagine the experience of disappearing into a peal of thunder.

That night I have difficulty sleeping. My wife snores. The neighbors host an all-night garage party. My muscles feel flaccid and raw.

Air escapes my lips and fragments into innumerable counterparts, daring me to disambiguate it...

Paraprosdokian

Nobody laughed during my set, but Johnny liked it. Afterwards he invited me over for a conversation.

"Fuck," I said, "off."

Johnny was insistent, maniacal. I felt embarrassed for him. I braced myself for a spectacle of revolt.

The revolt never came.

Reluctantly I sat down and began speedtalking like a dope fiend, interrupting Johnny whenever he asked me a question, telling shitty jokes, and adjudicating the meek.

He became uncomfortable. The audience became uncomfortable. I became uncomfortable and veered into linguistic territory that belonged in a gothic romance novel.

Johnny offered me a crumpled cigarette. "Those damn cigarettes," he quipped. Everybody laughed.

I confiscated the entire pack and smoked half of it. "I don't feel anything." I waited. "I still don't feel anything. What's next?"

BATTLE WITHOUT HONOR OR HUMANITY

That evening, at a political rally in the Flak District for the antimonarchist nominee, I gave a speech on the history of the party, its evolution and biodiversity, speaking into the microphone in a register that bordered on screaming, but not screaming. My conclusion was my thesis: "Echoes are not mere exercises in deception."

The bodyguards rushed me offstage and dragged me to the cellar. I exchanged pleasantries with the administration, then revealed this slice of life: "Oftentimes people will ask me, 'Hey, are you really that good?' I pause dramatically before replying in a polite, unaffected tone. 'Well, if I tell you I'm good, probably you will say that I'm boasting. But if I tell you I'm no good, you know I'm lying.'"

Everybody agreed that the repercussions of the slice of life were non-negotiable, the content itself innocuous, if plagiarized.

"Essentially we are dealing with a no-frills roman à clef," remarked the alleged ringleader, as if to assure his colleagues that cultural imperialism died with the modernists. I reminded him that my soul was crashproof. This confused every listener within range of my vocal processors long enough for me to drink most of the wine and get away with it.

Then:

I tested the legs on the latest rendition of an apostate New Zealand sauvignon blanc. I took a mindful sip and allowed the wine to soak into the carpet of my taste buds. A board of directors watched me expectantly, the turrets of their foreheads broad and moist and etched with grief.

Paraprosdokian

I delivered my verdict and slipped aside.

Downtown I ran into an old friend. He recognized me immediately and assured me that we had once been close.

His pink, bloated face didn't look familiar.

A long swath of acne ran from his brow to his cheek. He made no effort to conceal it.

I smelled marijuana and sex wax.

We discussed the past in animated tones. On several occasions my friend teetered on the knifepoint of epiphany only to backslide into worn and fabled doldrums. I took advantage of the conversation's peripeteia and faked a Charlie horse. He hailed an EMT and I pushed him out of the ambulance en route to the hospital. Mnemonic footage of him rolling across the asphalt like a kicked spintop will haunt me forever.

I allowed the paramedics to give me a sedative. They recognized me from TV. I signed and personalized their ledgers, then pushed them out of the vehicle. I got behind the wheel, second-guessed my actions, second-guessed them again (as always), and leapt out of the vehicle.

The vehicle countered its own redundancy and volte-faced across the gleaming rails.

Segue into rogue and irksome territory... Scent-texts from the Childhood Era echoed through the red leaves. Image of a house. A room. A sill. All of it reinforced by the music of dead genii.

Through a window in the Yellow Room I saw two teenagers toilet-papering the weeping willow tree in my front yard. A boy and a girl. They had done an adequate job already. I could tell they were in heat and exfoliating libidinal energy. Nonetheless I got my throwing stars and burst out the front door and started slinging the weapons, arms pumping like timelapsed ratchets. I had only intended to frighten the teenagers but I hit the boy in the thigh and the girl in the shoulderblade. They went down screaming for their mothers. The next day one of these headlines appeared in the news:

> HOMEOWNER SAVES TREE BY
> MANHANDLING RIFFRAFF
>
> COMEDIAN ATTACKS HELPLESS
> TEENAGERS WITH THROWING STARS

It could have been either one; TMZ is whimsical. As always, the result was the same: me leaning against a brick wall drawing smoke from a clove cigarette into an easy smile. The scene is shot is black-and-white monochrome and you can see an accrual of fire escapes and smokestacks in the background, blurred for added effect. A DVD copy of my latest film, *How to Kill a Wraith with Your Long and Capable Fingers*, rests snugly yet somehow precariously in the front pocket of my leisure jacket.

For my next trick, I burned a $500 pair of athletic shoes. It was a ceremonial affair. I had accomplished a great height, straddling the dome of a basilica in Florence. It was noon but I felt like Nietzsche at twilight. A mad swill of luminaries, non-luminaries and paparazzi teemed in the streets below as I gesticulated at the sky and called God a liar with a bullhorn. Then I yanked the shoes out of

Paraprosdokian

a sack, tossed them off the basilica and razed them with a flamethrower in mid-air. They fell burning into the crowd. Several people caught fire. I adjusted the bullhorn to full-throttle and said, "Burn! Burn! Burn!"

Somebody put out the flames with a fire extinguisher.

I escaped via dirigible. I always employ a dirigible when I'm on the lam. Nothing fancy. None of those elaborate steampunk contraptions. Just a high-powered balloon with an ion-propelled sphincter.

I went into seclusion. Multimedia death threats found me. This isn't unusual.

I emerged from seclusion and pressed on.

My agent set up a performance for me in northern Canada. I don't mind Canada when I'm up there in the tundra. Urban matrices are another plateau.

I told my agent I didn't believe in agents. Nor had I ever hired an agent. I fired him. He sued me. In court, an unassuming bailiff deployed rhetoric that neither the judge nor the jury could have predicted, let alone understood. A mistrial was declared and I attacked my agent in the bathroom of the courthouse, pounding his head against a sink. I crammed his body into a stall and left him in a frenzied REM state.

On my way to Canada, I received a phone call from my agent. "It's your agent," he intoned. "I'll meet you at the Liverpool."

"The Liverpool. In Liverpool?"

"Yeah. The Liverpool in Liverpool. You know, the pub. There are pubs in England. Don't be late. Goddamn it if you're late I'm going to be really upset! We need to talk. I'll be at the bar drinking the cheap stuff. Carlsberg, mainly. No liquor. It costs too much and they measure the pours like shitbird chemists."

I upgraded to business class and flew to Liverpool. I got drunk on the plane and did my routine in the aisle. I don't think anybody laughed but I couldn't be sure. After an hour or so, a flight attendant gave me a sedative. I slept the rest of the way.

I awoke in mid-stride, woozy but stable. The dirt road wound through the village like a flattened clockspring. Outside an inn two figures traded raucous verbal blows. Villagers observed the skirmish from a stationed distance. I wondered if I should keep going or join the crowd.

Intuition told me: "Wait for the next dream."

We waited for three days and nothing happened. I got hungry once and ate something. I don't know what. Possibly a frozen TV dinner. I procured it from the 1960s and devoured it on a fold-out table with hollow brass legs. My father danced with a shadow in the corner, dipping it into the light of a 1920s ballroom and revealing the shadow as my nascent mother, sad and haunted.

We continued to plunge into history.

The ringleader's hair sunk into her jawline. She had birdlike limbs and made birdlike gestures. I was attracted to her. She indoctrinated the wives of new families who moved into the neighborhood by way of a complicated hazing process that involved removing the clothes, getting on all fours, and easing backwards onto the cock of one "Bryan Hendersen," a pie-faced gallant from Tennessee. Bryan had the option of penetrating the wives anally or

Paraprosdokian

vaginally depending on several factors, ranging from an individual wife's angle of repose to the tilt of Bryan's erection, but in light of such factors, whether he went one way or the other wasn't so much an option (i.e., an act of free will) as a predetermined matter of course.

My wife was among Bryan's partners, although she denied it, standing naked in the hallway above the stairs, arms spread across the banister, legs folded and bent at the knees in the wrong direction, like a prehistoric insect, but the ringleader was adamant, assuring me that my wife did in fact "slide her asshole onto the weathervane," an expression that rattled my core and continued for more than an hour in a non-diminishing echo.

Later I confronted Bryan at a café west of the Gun Lake Casino. He was friendly and reminded me that we had taken several classes together in college, among them Astronomy and Business Mathematics. I didn't remember. He asked me what I had been up to since college and I didn't remember. "This happens a lot," I assured him, concentrating on the sound of my voice.

It sounded familiar.

Crennelated, I progressed backwards throughout the narrative of my life in a lightningbolt staccato of motion sensory deprivation.

This isn't accurate.

Johnny said, "There was that time Betty and I did Adam and Eve. The Monkeys stood offstage with their instruments as if they were hiding from a madman. They had such magnificent hair. That was a glorious time."

He lit a cigarette.

He lit another cigarette.

And died of emphysema, head slamming into the desktop like a gavel. The audience gasped and clawed for the exits as blood poured out of Johnny's mouth and splashed onto the lacquered floor of the set. Nobody had expected such an abrupt and graphic departure. Nobody ever does.

Emissary

A wide gully divides the lake house from the perimeter. An emissary throws himself across it and lands on a bay window, cracking the glass. He sticks there like a starved leech. He groans.

His companions are far less human and immediately threaten the interior landscape.

I stab at the crisp saladflakes with a fork, retrieving nothing, and consider the prospect of building memories. Confined to the house, I have not built a memory in years.

First: backstory.

Second: sensoria.

Third: cognition.

Fourth: storage.

A memory ejects from the sphincter of the equation like anaphora from a spleen.

The process implodes.

The process recommences.

The emissary disrupts the process, hammering the ceramic tiles of the kitchen with a mallet. Somehow he got inside.

He attracts an audience quickly and within minutes upends the social foundation of the lake house.

I respond with vitriol but eventually spiral into booze-and-drug-induced self-absorption.

The surf sighs as small waves exhale onto the beach.

I go to the atrium and chase the brides. I catch one, contemplate strangulation, and set her free.

This is life, I remind myself. This is real.

In a guest bedroom, the emissary accumulates a viral cult following; fanatics repeatedly fail to exorcise the crude specter of his identity from their animal cores.

Tabula rasa. And yet my awareness persists.

It isn't enough.

The god in the machine suffers from narcolepsy and forgets about "Emissary" by the time it wakes up. Instead it remembers a nonexistent line of flight and conjures it into being.

Everybody but me dies like a storm, evaporating into the Blue Slum.

I go to the lakefront.

I haven't been outside for years.

Two grizzled motorists have abandoned their vehicles in the surf. I don't see the motorists and inspect the vehicles for imperfections and general utility.

Alarmed, I look behind me and snatch at the air. Nobody's there. I return my attention to the vehicles.

Emissary

The motorists blindside me.

They drag me screaming through the sand and the seaweed and the mollusks.

As I experience the drama and agony of the transgression, I recall a conversation that I had with my mistress at dinner last week on the veranda.

"It is an ontological prerequisite that I fuck you in the something-or-other," I said, clouds passing overhead at an impossible velocity.

"What?" replied the mistress.

"It is an ontological prerequisite that I fuck you in the something-or-other," I repeated.

"That's what I thought you said," replied the mistress.

... The motorists get tired and drape my body across a bed of pebbles.

The seafroth tastes like sake, hot and strong. I stop screaming, shoot to my feet, fall down, get back up and start throwing punches.

I miss.

I miss.

I hit one of them, killing him: his jaw explodes like a piñata and something evil pours from the hole in his face as he drops to his knees and implodes into a nascent ball-peen abdomen.

Adrenalized, I go after the other one.

We struggle.

And he says, "Never underestimate the idiocy of the common man." That piques my interest and we strike up a conversation. He asks who I am and I refer to myself as an emissary.

BATTLE WITHOUT HONOR OR HUMANITY

"My memory," I add, making an explosive gesture with my fingers...

Flames ravage a building on the silver coastline.

There is no smoke.

The image conjures my childhood with piercing accuracy. All of it.

I feel as if it's happening right now.

When I was two.

When I was three.

And so on.

And then, on my eighth birthday, an emissary arrived at the party and took me aside.

Nobody tried to prevent him.

He pulled me out of the bathroom window—I knocked my chin against the sill and bit my tongue—and we stood on the roof and observed the shingles.

Suddenly he took me by the ears as if my head were a trophy.

"Only in retrospect do we recognize the surplus of our identity," he said. He was serious. "We must conquer the steppes before we can become nomads," he added. I don't think I've ever seen a more serious expression on a human being's face.

But it might not have been the expression.

It might have been his stance.

Possibly it was something inside of me that had nothing to do with the emissary. I perceived a seriousness in him that was little more than a projection of my own vanguard. But I was just a boy. And memory is unreliable, especially when you've lost it.

Emissary

At this point I think the emissary wanted to hurt me. Everybody was watching us from inside the bathroom.

Mom and dad.

Sisters and brothers and relatives and friends.

All of their faces pushed together into a fretful mosaic.

The emissary made his move . . . and lost his footing.

Gravity seemed to take him by the ankles, drag him across the roof, and yank him down, down, down . . .

It was a long way.

I ran to the roof's edge, hoping to see him land. Too late. He slept on the sidewalk like a broken puppet. His arms and legs had come off and were all twisted in the wrong directions.

There was no blood.

Bibliomancer

A fat librarian slams into the periphery. She has married the role: frizzled gray hair, coke bottle spectacles, judgmental yellow grin, acid-washed rawhide, long faux-pearl necklace, plus-sized dress that looks more like a window curtain in an Old Folks parlor, all complemented by the razorsharp ethics of a thoroughbred Prude...

We get in a fight. I take a swing and scrape my knuckles against a sidebar. She leans in with a powerful forearm and clips me on the jaw, momentarily paralyzing me. The elbow is calloused and rough, like crumpled sandpaper.

The blow draws blood.

Towering shelves of leatherbound survival manuals call the atmosphere into question. Addicted to clichés, I remove a volume and open it to the copyright page. I read the publishing information, voraciously, waiting for jackdaws to descend on a traumatic hotbed. They don't come. The librarian releases a second volley. This time I'm ready and I duck out of the way and lunge at her with a two-handed mallet. I find purchase between the shoulderblades. She hammers the asphalt, cracking it, and her limbs snap backwards into her core.

The reel unspools in the wake a fever dream. The monotony of celluloid, the tyranny of evil birds.

... A paranoid skaterat perceives herself as an intellectual and finagles her way into the classroom. Professor Superzero indulges her until she allows him to fuck her, then delicately explains that her wires are crisscrossed, her dogmatisms unoccupied; she must storm the video fairgrounds and never go back to Attica. The professor adds, "I am not intimidated by your skaterat morality. Go away. Sprinkle your klonopin dust in somebody else's nasal cavity. Your teeth are yellow and your bones show through the rind. Disavowal is the price of life, but I assure you, my subjectivity conquered the objective world long ago, and I apologize in advance when I say that your preternatural delusions are your own affair. Skate or die."

We arrive at the entrance to prediscursive Certainty. This matrix contravenes the impossible. Brass instruments die a quick death and a towering stone door yawns open. I ready myself for an apocalypse with the same vigilance and fortitude that I would apply to a hangnail. Whatever happens—the destruction of everything, an epidermal imperfection, anything in between—I will deflect the atrocity and set fire to all of Voltaire's gardens.

Beyond the perimeter, a man sits in a corner and speaks into the magneto generator of a wooden hand-cranked telephone affixed to the wall. He repeats this dictum with the relativity of a cheap metronome: "The unconscious is structured like a language." He does not have eyelids and I may or may not be mistaking myself as the target of his half-baked gaze.

Idle, he shows me his head and stares blankly at the artifact, gesturing towards Futurity.

I enter the long gable and listen to a twenty-minute paper on autofeminism. The woman who reads the paper may be the librarian; for the moment, at least, her flesh defies her identity. Every seat is occupied and I have to stand in the aisle. Afterwards we drink stale coffee and eat dry scones and talk about the aisle (how it veers to the left, how it isn't like other aisles, how it wouldn't exist in the absence of chair assemblages, etc.). A professor of business ethics approaches me. "Welcome to Public Health Terrorism 305," he announces, as if occupying a lectern. I can smell the aftershock on his breath. "As you know, there are significant student fees for this course. Fees upwards of 500 dollars, I say. You need to pay for your guns. You must recognize the dynamism of my unease. Also, remember the golden rule: always go to bed on an empty stomach and never eat carbohydrates after six o'clock."

"I am not a student," I explain. "And I have not tasted a carbohydrate in over thirty years." I lift my shirt and expose the Lacanian Real . . .

I walk backwards into my dorm room. The timelapse accelerates and decelerates, ebbs and flows. I have two roommates. One of them is a student. I don't detect his presence at first, and when I do, anxiety and dread infect me like a worldview. He sits on a wooden stool and holds a shaved head in his hands. "What did I do?" I ask in backwardspeak. "I know I did something. Otherwise you wouldn't be here." He falls asleep and slips off of the stool. He might have been sleeping in the first place. I wake him and he gets up and directs me towards the cafeteria at a harrowing pace.

A writer pries his way into the mise en scène. Calmly a gunman steps into view and shoots him in the head. Broken polaroids splatter against the wall. "No writers allowed," says the gunman.

In the cafeteria, I make small talk with the cook, then order 10 mg of Flexeril, 10 mg of Xanax, half an ounce of marijuana, a vial of crack and an eight-ball of cocaine. I swallow all of the pills, smoke all of the pot, mainline the rock and snort the blow. Sensing death, I seek out the nearest bathtub and turn on the water. Celluloid pours out of the faucet like bad honey. I submerge myself and push all of the air from my lungs. I lay in the tub with eyes open for an undisclosed length of time . . . then get out and dry off, feeling refreshed despite mild agonal respirations, clogged arteries and cardiac arrhythmia.

"The drugs have worn off," I explain to a chambermaid, wooing her. She turns from the window with a quick jerk and exposes herself as the librarian. The rolling flags of her cheeks frame an evil grin.

She utters something that I promptly internalize, repress and blot out.

I remind her: "I do drugs because of the people I meet. Especially the ones I want to meet. Nobody I have ever liked on paper has appealed to me as a human being. In fact, the more I like them on paper, the more I despise them *dans la chair.*"

"*En chair,*" she explains.

The synapses hit their respective bullseyes and she realizes I am nothing short of an electromagnetic earthfucker. She tries to jump off of the balcony, but I catch her by the apron, and I punch her in the kidneys until I get tired and can't lift my arms. Splayed out on the carpet like a great, mangled crab, the librarian gasps for air, quivering in weird places, as I stride onto the balcony and admire the view. Beneath me, the colorful streets of Nice fall into a nude beach populated by old, hairy Europeans in thongs.

The afternoon threads into midnight and I can't see anything or anybody.

In an attempt to find the sun, I buy a first class ticket to Miami and fall asleep in the lobby of the hotel. A bellhop negotiates suitcases that I have filled with quicksand in an attempt to dissuade thieves and baggage handlers. Eternity stretches across the coastline. The commander-in-chief's disabled brother is a cook in the hotel. Time after time he exits the kitchen, making faces and noises, and the commander-in-chief must escort him into a back room, by the elbow, firmly, with a concerned smile.

I awake.

Roosting on tall chairs, logicians in flower-patterned cruisewear have surrounded me.

The commander-in-chief stands next to us. He asks what we think about the state of pop music and the direction it should go in. Plainly intimidated, the logicians mete out articulate, quickfire responses in need of revision and more thoughtfulness. I don't know the answer to his question and slip aside.

The next time I wake it is to the music of apocalyptic alarm trumpets. "Forty seconds ago, the earth moved," says a voice in German. And then, in English: "*Wir werden total gebumst.*" We run out of the hotel and try to get to higher ground, scrambling up escarpments and buttes and fjälls, but Sweden has already conquered the sky; the resultant tsunami defies normative conceptions of acromegaly and I acknowledge the futility of escape. I stand in the grass and wait to drown.

Before birth, I worried about this moment.

Anxiestentialism.

Anxiety precedes existence.

Essence as a choleric adenoid.

"Wither-skeleton" (the antithesis of "skeleton").

The waters roll over me and drag me across the tundra and I tumble into a distant oubliette blinking on the rim of Creation . . . The door is ajar. Quietly I escape and kill the first person I encounter on the street, a good Samaritan who offers me a ride. Staring at the corpse, I perceive the Samaritan as the librarian.

Three plainclothes officers collect me and drag me back to jail, as if expecting my insurrection, but the warden tells them to let me go. "She's dead," he explains, "and this man has already been punished." We smoke a cigar and talk about Africa and then I release myself on my own veiled recognizance.

BATTLE WITHOUT HONOR OR HUMANITY

Finally I enter the library. I begin to unpack it. Crates and torn papers cover the floor. Dust surges through the crooked stacks, pooling in open knots. The staff doesn't know what to do. I put the communications director in a headlock and knock him out with a cravat soaked in chloroform that I press against his nose. The walls of the control room shift and slide and lock in and out of place like a puzzlebox. I use the intercom system to remind everybody: "Such a man is speaking to you. On closer scrutiny he proves to be speaking only about himself." Occasionally I pin down a worker by the arms and hammer my fists against his face and chest until he stops calling me sir. This manner of conduct seeps into the ecosphere. It prompts unspeakable flowers to wilt on the vine while moratoria rise from the wounds of open, informative graves . . .

Autocracy

The rector ushers my father and me to a fjord where we must formally present a valediction to one of the rector's less meaningful subordinates, standing there on behalf of the rector himself, a surrogate-of-all-trades, for the inauguration of the holiday season. He is nearly half my size, with a slight hunchback, grizzled pewter mustache, and a purposeful flicker in his eyes. He grips my elbow firmly with one hand and strokes my spine with the other. "This is the best thing for everybody," he utters in a pan-seared Russian drawl.

"Thank you, Rector." Nodes of synthetic pain dart to the surface of my skin whenever I speak. It hasn't always been this way. And yet I talk now more than I used to.

My father hasn't spoken in decades. I forgot what his voice sounded like long ago.

"Behind the word is chaos," says my father, quoting a dead killjoy. The apparatus of his frame has become more of a stockroom object than a human thing, tempting users to hang tools on it before the prospect of interaction even enters their scope of reckoning. I nod in affirmation of his broken silence. Melancholy, the rector signals a punisher from the Bronze Turret and my father suffers a fasttime blow to the kidneys. Blood races down the back of his thighs like insects on fire . . .

The rector apologizes. As we move forward, he metes out additional encouragement in clipped, controlled soliloquies. I study a red mole on the shoulderblade of the man in front of me. Finally the line dwindles and my father and I face the effigy of the rector, who has left my side.

"I am the rector," says the effigy. "I hereby sentence you to a means of escape."

My father emits a liquid croak and we take a tour of the refractory before leaving and walking thirty miles across savannahs and flatlands until we reach the tall house on the grassy, hilly frontiers . . . Halfway there my father dies. I carry him onto the porch and prepare him for burial with a first-aid kit. As I clean wounds and plug outlets, his last word, relegated to a save station somewhere in the hard palate, flees the wet cavern of his intellect.

"Father." The word bounds across the landscape with the soft antagonism of a lunar rover.

Immediately I am drawn to a soldier in the valley. We run towards the enemy, muskets in tow, passing a flask of dirty whiskey back and forth while assuring one another that pain operates more or less like a troll: feed it and eventually it will feed on you. The soldier is fat, with rumpled eyebrows, wearing exaggerated civilian attire

Autocracy

and Calvary headgear. I can't tell if this is the American Revolution, the Civil War, or World War II: the bright colors of the British bleed into racingstripe confederate regalia that bleeds into Nazi chic armbands and logos and Luftwaffe dreams ... Struck by an electromagnetic projectile device, the soldier devolves before my eyes into an ur-man, boneless and primordial, but spry. He flows into a bush and either disappears into thin air or succumbs to a weird symbiotic process of herbal assimilation.

I hide in an outhouse and wait for the battle to end. I study and assess the mélange of voices I hear between gunfire, indulging the accents of battered memories.

The outhouse door creaks open and I enter the studio that belongs to the lesser gods.

Errant directors dart back and forth across the floorboards in an orderly frenzy. All of the actors have been raptured. Residual costumes litter the place in hot clumps, steam rising from their sequined folds into the heavens. The directors sense my presence and surround me in a regimented square. They tell me to prepare for an audition, but I know they need me—I know everything about them, incidentally, their *modi operandi*, their dark secrets, their sordid histories and beveled futures—ontologies ripped open and elongated into spacetime worms— and I state my terms before administering an impromptu monologue that engages Shakespearean and Beckettian discourse in equal measure. I ignore my skin. Stupified, the directors call attention to the hangmen lingering on the outpost. One false move and the hangmen will attack, swinging nooses like lassos. A deliberation ensues and hot words are traded for dejected underpinnings. Nothing is resolved.

As I hang up my coat, a windbreaker with the clergical facilities of an Edwardian snapjacket, a man (latino, thirty-something, emaciated yet well-groomed) steps beside me. He holds a burlap sack with a child in it. I recognize the man as the keeper of the Prism. He places the sack on a low-lying worktable and stomps on it, then picks it up and twists the drawstring, pulling it taut, and twirls the sack back and forth, from one hip to the other, violently, methodically, at skewed angles of incidence, destroying the child inside. He leaves the sack on the worktable and retreats into a storage elevator.

My anxiety describes itself with a bolt of elocution. Paralyzed, I wonder what to do. If I tell the police, the killer will likely hunt me down and dispatch my immediate family, a memory at best, but a family is a family. If I don't tell the police, I may be held in contempt, by the Law, and by society in general. Another factor races to the vanguard. According to the news broadcasts streaming overhead, the killer has never killed anybody before, i.e., nobody has ever witnessed him commit a killing. A timelapse of his deeds runs backwards across the screens and no incriminating evidence comes to fruition.

I recall the ninth of September. Something ominous happened on that "fateful day," as the newsman refers to it, over and over, until the rhetoric usurps the authority of the teleprompter and I can only refer to my diary, which I began to keep shortly after my father and I were incarcerated in the refractory. I scan the entries and they seem foreign, obscure—articulate, but written by another author. For a moment I doubt the existence of my body, spreading my fingers and scrutinizing their terrific span. A wide clerk in a three-piece suit interrupts me with a dramatic, democratic promise. Spitting image of Boss Tweed on the Boardwalk...

"The nature of war implicates the push-button dynamics of certain overpowering stimuli," intones the wide clerk. "Your contribution to the system of human corruption will stain the future like a crater in the ozone layer. You will, in fact, become the ozone layer—simultaneously all-encompassing and nonexistent—a god in the making—a god at the end of time."

Spatial conundrums exit my body in expanding ripples, searching for the joy of concentric precision.

The impact delivers me to the basement where the enemy performs a sacred rite upon a man who may or may not be the rector. The technique descended from an old Viking technology of fear and liberation. Called the blood eagle, it entails cracking open the sternum and removing the lungs, each of which are nailed to sideboards running just above the victim's body so that, in effect, the lungs, still connected to the chest cavity by various sinews and tendrils, resemble wings.

"He had been enjoying a glass of wine when we found him," says the enemy, cleaning his arms and hands with a wet towel. "I think he expected us to join in the merriment. He certainly didn't expect to die. Who does? This is the best thing for everybody. For some folks, it is the worst thing. But things are always relative. One only hopes that things pan out. If they don't, we must spread our cheeks and endure the Cock of Life."

The purview works.

Intuition transports me into an historical claptrap, and I finish the rector's drink. It has no taste. It slides off of my tongue and down my throat like synthetic oil. I express regret, formally, loudly, and my skin doesn't react; I realize it hasn't reacted for years.

I spend the rest of my holiday waiting to be reborn and unborn . . . Then I am preborn, and I don't go back to the refractory. I drink too much beer at a pub and end up stumblebum, waddling down a wooden staircase, the creaking of which, given my frame of mind, I don't take into consideration. The lord of the manor awakens and calls the police and they arrest me and lock me in the hangtank. I place my nose against the plastic wall. I run my fingertips across the breath holes. Another drunk claims to be my father. He looks like my father in healthier days, despite the glazed eyes and bristled face. He wiggles his toes as if to assure me of the inevitability of genetic inscription.

Nearby an atomic bomb test site becomes fully operational. The building shakes and the walls crack open . . .

Fingers trembling, I take two acetametaphine and two aspirin and swallow the pills with a cup of coffee. I read the paper. I consider going to work. Things become unfathomably normal, appallingly real at this point. I almost forget about what happened, about history altogether, my own, and that which unfolded in the objective world. And then I do forget . . . My headache dissipates and the coffee goes cold, stale, even as I secure the cup.

Directeur

1

"This is the thing. We get a monkey to direct the next installment of *Planet of the Apes*. I don't just mean any monkey. I mean, like, a really angry monkey, one that's been in a cage for awhile and experimented on, or maybe just heckled by zoogoers. Who's with me!"

Everybody stares at the production manager.

After some back and forth, it's decided that a monkey is the way to go. "Monkeys are all always funny," concluded the executive producers. "Something about their unbridled, free-range humanity."

The monkey does a good job.

Nobody expected such a dynamic performance.

At the test screening, the senior editor introduces an unedited 8-hour-long version of the new treatment and concludes with the following remarks: "Very well.

The thing about death is everybody gets to do it. I mean, everybody dies. Like so."

He achieves an endgame in realtime.

The camera fixes on the horrified outcries of the audience in the front row, documenting the bloodspatter that soaks their cheeks, their teeth, the glistening whites of their eyes . . .

The director doesn't show up. He didn't even appear on the set of the film, insisting on shooting the whole thing via digital interlink from a remote African hut. Specific location unknown. The end-product transcends even the wildest expectations of viewers and critics. Unlike the first installment, the film doesn't win an award, but this is out of the question: films involving simian extrapolation (viz., chimpsploitation) no longer win awards, not even for makeup and special effects. Something about the iniquity of anthropomorphism . . .

2

I book a flight from Nairobi to Ohio.

It takes me longer than I expect to get to Nairobi. I book another flight en route and then book another one upon arrival, three weeks later.

The atmosphere smells of legumes and body odor.

Ohio. Baggage claim.

A man in a cheap suit approaches me from across the airport and attempts to guilt me into voting, assuming I have established residency in the state. He unfolds a document and shows me my voting history, which not

Directeur

only assures me that I have never cast a vote for any candidate, but that I have never even generated brainwaves indicating a single thought regarding the voting process. This latter piece of information, the man explains, was obtained via electroencephalogram administered from a geosynchronous satellite over Mozambique.

"It is my right to vote," I remind him. "Just as it is my right not to vote."

He castigates me with poise and impunity. People start to look at us.

Without responding, I remove a handheld shotputter from my suitcase, vintage, a Wizard 8 mm wind-up turret movie camera, made in Japan in 1959, and I begin to film the man. The wrinkles in his suit remind me of jungle ravines (from the macroscopic) and fruit grooves (from the microscopic). Terrified, I pan down and zoom in on his shoes, considering what soundtrack would work best with the way in which I move the lens across the spoiled leather. When I retain enough footage, I put the camera away, scribble my vote on a slip of paper and hand it to the man, telling him to give it to the right people, assuring him that it is a mark of my dire humanity. Perhaps the most important mark anybody can make.

My vote cast, I slip between the cracks and repel down the vines, the creepers, the lianas into a Third World . . .

3

"The doctor prescribed me an anti-psychotic," he intones. "Just this very morning. The name of the drug escapes me.

Don't be worried—the dosage is low. But I need something to help me with the fear of death. Thanatophobia. I want to believe in God, but I don't. I believe in the extinguishment of consciousness. Oblivion. Nothingness. I have episodes in which I race to the conclusion of my life, the tail-end of my spacetime worm, and realize, hopelessly, palpably, that I, like everyone and everything that has ever lived, will fucking die!" He pauses to stow away the broken clocksprings, the popped weasels, the unboxed jacks. "Benzos don't work anymore. Even in high quantities. I can take 10 mg of Ativan and not feel a thing. Likewise with lava. I can drink it and nothing happens. Yes, the stuff that comes out of volcanoes. I'm not kidding! Unfortunately I am morbidly serious. Very likely I am immortal. And yet there it is—my existential dread."

Darkened claps pursue the monologue, clawing for evolution, but there's too much Fear.

Fear's worst crime is the incrimination of all spectacles of momentum.

Barn doors swing open as if bulldozed but nothing comes out. Everybody chews on their lips. Surely something will come out. Some kind of barn animal, right? A stampede. Perhaps a Great Flood.

There's nothing in the barn.

Even meaningful redundancy can't placate our angst. Inevitably, we dovetail into meaninglessness.

Media culture as a hindrance to remembering that we possess an inner being, a spirit. The ordinariness of it all.

To use the essence as a template.

Rough and raw.

Directeur

Dripping with gender and ectoplasm.

When one attempts to comb the hair of one's arm, one experiences difficulties. Shave the hair and annul the difficulties. Shave the hair and do away with the comb altogether. This may seem like a modest proposal but in fact it is a means of propulsion that may be superimposed onto any aspect of one's existence.

Long footpath here. It tapers into the brush and the protagonist of the nightmare swings atop the Gateway Arch in St. Louis. He can see his reflection in the mirrored surface. Far beneath him, elderly proletarians hobble back and forth through the turnstiles of the casino. He removes a computer from a backpack in order to document the experience. It will make a great screenplay, he thinks. Bad weather up there, though, and it's difficult to type; the wind seems insistent on keeping his gnarled fingers from the keyboard. He worries about productivity and charts out a new plan. Just as he is about to enact it, the computer blows away and falls into the Mississippi River. Devastated, he climbs into a porthole and takes the elevator to the ground, gibbering about his loss to confounded tourists. At ground zero he storms into the casino and kicks over card tables and yanks the levers off of slot machines and strangles a pit boss and finally the cops show up in anti-riot vehicles and arrest him. He escapes into the ventilation system, overdosing on oxygen and the Ides of Ben-Gay. Consciousness impales him as he emerges onto the stage of eternity. An audience of neophyte actors and misdirected film buffs heatedly await a soliloquy, or a speech, or mere directions on how to succeed in the industry. They perceive him as a Duke of Hazzard and expect Big Things.

"Mrrrk," he says, thinking about the computer. Then he climbs onto the lectern and begins to massage the microphone likes a mons pubis.

The production manager commands a troupe of furies to contain the director in a wooden box. A cargo truck backs onto the stage and they hurl the box into an empty 40-foot container and slam and lock the doors. The truck idles. The audience awaits a departure.

The truck idles.

The truck idles.

The truck idles.

The truck idles.

The truck idles.

The truck idles.

The truck idles.

The truck idles.

The truck idles.

The truck idles.

The truck idles.

The truck idles.

The truck idles.

The truck idles.

The truck runs out of gas.

By this time, the audience has either gone home or, in most cases, lived out their lives and died.

The sun sets and never rises again, but the stagelights stay on and they never go off. Weeds push through cracks in the hardwood. Unexpectedly an entire savannah

Directeur

stretches into the distance. Rich canopies of herbs and flood-meadows shelter the mean spots, the dark places. This happens and soon we forget about the director, realizing that, all along, he was more or less a non-intrusive coalescence of desire and disinclination empowered by absence, presence, and variable quantities of liminality.

Virulence

Stark phalanges exposed themselves to the liquid night and a crenellation rose from the sand like a fist. "The subject has been weaponized," said a voice in an evacuated contralto. Fingers of electricity pulsed within the gas cloud whenever it spoke . . .

This prologue delivered the victims to the Waiting Room, a makeshift version of a low-income garage: mechanical undesirables stacked in a corner, an attic string dangling from a trapdoor in the ceiling, oceanic cobwebs, etc., etc. . . . Beyond the perimeter, a courtesan practiced burlesque dance moves in a narrow cage, breasts spilling from either side of a Naugahyde halter-top.

An addict leaned over a fold-out table. I passed him a pipe. He put it to his lips, tentatively, then smoked it and exclaimed, "Jesus Christ! Living without this hooch has been like losing a dear old friend every day of my life. Welcome back. It's good to have a friend." He smoked the pipe again, this time to the core. Thereafter he continued to inhale air, sucking at the stem with increasing angst. "More!" he barked.

Roarke entered, stage right. Unaccustomed to this manner of interscape, he walked sideways across the Waiting Room and exited via the Retinal Chamber. A stigmatism marked his vision in the left eye; he could actually see it if he closed the lids and concentrated, deflecting idle trailers and blotches of religiosity.

Knock at the door. Roarke opened it and let in Agent Zed, who strode forward and took him by the shoulders. "The baby! Where's the baby!" He tossed Roarke aside and I handed him the baby, which, in the words of Agent Zed himself, he "confiscated without prejudice, malice, or forethought."

Roarke regained composure and acted in response. Cradling the baby in one arm, Agent Zed fought off his assailant with the other arm, easily, until Roarke had been "defeated without cunning, dash, or autonomia."

The scene dissolved into savannah and wind . . .

Back in the Waiting Room, a vintage black-and-white television set fizzled to life. A central dot expanded to the four corners of the screen in an oblong circle. For a moment, the virtual shibboleth threatened to implode. Then an anti-smoking commercial featuring Yul Brynner came on. In a black, tight-collared shirt, with token bald head and elfish, possibly prosthetic ears, he looked into the camera and, voice deep and grating, a mutant basso from some evicted nightmare demonstrating the faintest trace of a weathered Russian accent, said, "Now that I am gone, I tell you: DON'T SMOKE." The commercial ran again. Again and again—an endless chain of guidance and foreboding.

. . . anxiety stamps itself onto the lapel of the Backyard Industrialist like a heraldic fleur-de-lis. He proceeds across the construction beam and surveys the black-and-white metropolis from two miles skywards. No acrophobia, but the prospect of a miserable future cuts him to the quick, and he steps off the edge and falls into the past tense, where everybody technically belongs . . . at which point the weaponized subject cried out for his father. Again.

Herr Moritz exclaimed, "It's not my fault you exist in a universe of mutant appliances and acausal gizmos. Your technophobia is your own affair. I have never willfully projected orthopedics into your midst. Or, for that matter, into your person. I always told you that you were a good boy. Every day, like. Here. Let me adjust that chinstrap. There. That's better. Wait. This clubfoot prosthetic is all wrong. How do you expect it to produce the requisite synaptic charges, cathexes, and pyrotechnic magnetisms? Imagine Lord Byron in such a contraption. How might his poetry have suffered . . . or evolved. Don Juan may have emerged as the first literary Martian, assuming, of course, that a sufficient and rightwise population of Burroughsian *femmes violeurs* inhabited the red planet. Now. Let's have that microscope, then. Right. Bend over, if you please. Thank you. Just remember, boy: God is as much a friend to you as a cauterized wound. One way or another, everything heals, if only by the art of death. Tabula rasa. The art of death wipes all blank slates clean . . ."

Virulence

I erased chalkdust from the blackboard and flipped a switch, flooding the room with pixels of admission. Cathode rays hummed to life and paralyzed all viewers within reach. Onscreen the President of the United States deflected questions during an outdoor media briefing in a stylized fit of verbal wuxia pan. He stood tall above the mic. Stage left, the First Lady stumbled into view, with scarecrow hair and shotgun mascara running from the eyes like leaning towers of babel. She had not swallowed another case of beer. Idle, sober derangement was the thing. I secured a can of Budweiser and ordered a secret service agent to deliver it to the Lady. He refused to partake in what amounted to "a demoralizing act of kindness," but a ray of sunlight caught the beer can just so, producing an eloquent glint in the Lady's eyes. With my assistance, soon she was shitfaced for real and the media briefing culminated in a kind of battle royal, the president exiting on a telescopic ladder dangling from a Marine One helicopter like a flaccid proboscis.

An ailing ex-president noted, "He's just an actor. It's not real."

Despite victory, Agent Zed continued to assail Roarke, as if to prove that he could do it, i.e., to show everybody that he was the kind of man who wasn't afraid to beat a man when he was down. Roarke put up a wretched fight, an overturned turtle or beetle defending himself, extremities flailing but with no apparent purpose other than to produce movement. This may or may not have upset Agent Zed, although the aspersions he cast became louder and more garbled, and he pummeled his victim with increasing brutality. According to my reading of his facial lexis, however, every new blow produced a calendar of regret, possibly mourning. I stepped forward to get a closer look, scrutinizing both men for good measure, and effectively collapsing the fourth wall. Aggravated, Agent Zed paused and said, "I can smell your breath. It reeks of desperation and cant."

"I suffer from pragmatism," I clarified.

Roarke died on the floor. Agent Zed made reservations at a preferred mausoleum and gave a bad eulogy. It sounded like this: "Space harbors an eternal guitar tab—a club hammers mankind's kettledrum between the whining high notes. It occurs to me that I know very little about death beyond various methods of dispatch and internment. The last intimate acquaintance of mine who died was my grandfather. I was just a boy and faith in God allowed me to negotiate the ordeal as if it never happened; Grandpa was in a better place, I told myself, and I was happy for him, even envious. Now this. What do thinking creatures do when loved ones pass into the infinite Zilch of oblivion? What can we do but embrace one of two things: fearsome disavowal or furious anger . . ."

I recollected the prototype I met in Mr. Vanderwoude's office, a kind of excrescent waiting room adjacent the Waiting Room. He introduced himself and I showed him photographs of me as a child. In one photo, I stood triumphant above a lattice of feather-strewn chickenwire, a pose accomplished shortly after chasing all of the hens from the coop. "I don't know why I like it so much," I mused. "Something about the innocence of it. And the horror."

Virulence

"I'm disappointed," replied the prototype, studying the photograph like an uncrackable code. "I wanted so much to enjoy this. I wanted. I sought. But I didn't find. It's not here. The grail. Not. No."

Still images drifted across the carpet, propelled by an artificial breeze.

Mr. Vanderwoude stood over seven feet tall. A devout Christian Reformed Dutchman and former "athletic director"—the script puts his biography in chronic jeopardy—he emitted the contaminant of Judgment from every pore, namely his eyes, two old, open wounds defined by two central pinpoints of superwhite light. He lingered near a closet. Every movement, however subtle or gesticulatory, was a dare.

I never escaped the reverie . . .

Roarke had been dead for days now. On a whim, a team of semi-drunk EMTs, none of them close relatives, exhumed the body and restarted his heart, chasing a provisional defibrillator with an atropine and adrenaline cocktail. Consciousness found him halfway through an apology for his life, arguing his case like a sidestreet lawyer disputing a speeding ticket. He spoke with an affected drawl and often repeated the word "stooge" without any apparent syntactic methodology or valence. Imagined jurors listened with simulated attentiveness, comprehension and sympathy, and when the defense rested, the audience calmly filed out of the courtroom into the lobby, hard rubber soles clacking against the marble floorplanks.

Presidency

"Is that the president's gun? Let me have it."

I reached out.

The bodyguard took the gun by its barrel and slammed the butt into my knuckles. A snare of pain ran up my forearm to the elbow.

I reprimanded the bodyguard and disarmed him.

The .357 Colt Python, standard-issue among national figureheads, even in third world countries since the passage of the BMS (Ballistic Mogadishu Sanction), had been souped-up over the years, with a solarized ammo uplink for effect and an amplified underlug for show. The trigger, too, had been manufactured with a polysynaptic alloy that wired the user's brain to the datasphere of the gun, giving the user the option to fire without actually pulling the trigger. An entirely bourgeois feature—little more than an *objet d'art* to brag about like a Picasso hanging above the fireplace. I liked it.

Presidency

"Give it back," said the bodyguard. "We're filming in infrared photonegative telekineticolor today with an eye to a werewolf point-of-view. Mind the White Lodge aesthetic and remember to speak backwards in standard mirror language. As always, events occur in outré-time."

I handed him the gun. Carefully he returned it to the velvet-lined, cherry wood humidor in which the president kept the weapon under supposed lock and key.

Beside the humidor was a picture of the president at the grand finale of last year's Stormgrade Mandible Classic; center-stage, with vein-encrusted arms flexed overhead and hands crunched into opposing fists, he struck a vacuum pose that accomplished an impressive latspread and abdominal rumblestrips while producing uncanny striations in the pectoralis minor. Hanging on the wall behind the desk was a much bigger picture of the president at the same competition striking a different pose that foregrounded the muscles of the scapula region. He had come in fifth. In more than one State of the Union address, he admitted that he couldn't do better, although, of course, he had no choice but to continue to train and compete throughout his final term. The best he could hope for was that competitors with genetic advantages and more experience would sustain injuries. In his first year of office, he ordered a hit on the world champion, but Donovan Ogg's death didn't resonate with him psychologically, and since then he treaded shallow waters when it came to bloodthirsty sportsmanship.

Currently the president stood at ease in front of the east door. His skin looked more orange than usual set against the white rose garden through the windows. His grin made the flowers look gray in comparison.

Everybody in the office expected the attack. I had been planning on it for weeks.

With fluid immediacy, I removed the gun from the humidor and pistolwhipped the bodyguard across the chin, once, dislocating the jaw; the undercarriage hung from his skull like a walletflap as he ogled me in dazed surprise and staggered backwards.

I shot him in the forehead and a hyperreal clump of gore exploded onto a bookshelf behind him. Proxies responded like stepped-on mousetraps. I shot them at haphazard, somewhat adrenalized intervals, maneuvering the mind-trigger in such a way that the bullets came out fifty, sixty at a time and nearly vaporized their targets, fabric, flesh and all.

I saved the last round for the president.

"You have misunderestimated me," he commanded, eyeballing me with raw indifference.

I shot him in the chest. His pectorals sagged and seemed to draw him to his knees, shattering the caps, and the bullethole screamed like a wraith. He tried to say something to me, then fell sideways into the hardwood floor as if knocked over by a rubber mallet.

The red phone rang.

I wiped my fingerprints from the gun with my tie, returned it to the humidor, contemplated my death, and picked up the receiver.

"Mr. President?" said a voice.

"This is me," I replied.

Presidency

"You have been nominated for an Academy Award. Congratulations."

"Thank you. This is a surprise. I wasn't in any movies this year. I'm not an actor. I only exist in reality."

"Nevertheless somebody will be over shortly to collect you. Remember to wash your hands."

I placed the receiver on the desk. I unmanned the receivers for the black and yellow phones. There was a collective disharmony followed by a numb flatline.

A poorly shaved Arab wearing a keffiyeh and a garish identity suit ushered me from the oval office to Gold's Gym. He promised to have me back before the arrival of the awards committee.

On the way there, he assured me that the phone call had been a purposeful fiction . . .

The overt reversion to the Golden Age of bodybuilding offset me. The equipment was ancient and limited mainly to kettlebells, dumbbells, barbells . . . No machines. Mirrors were scant and reflected images without bias or augmentation. This had to do with the lighting, too. Even the bodybuilders lacked the definition and bulk of modern politicians. It was as if I had been forced through the blowhole of a time warp.

Gripping 50 lb. dumbbells, I found an empty bench, sat on the end of it, and did a set of speedy alternating curls to failure. I was able to do more reps with my left arm, despite being right-handed. I attributed the anomaly to a stigmatism I incurred as a child. The subsequent pump in my biceps reminded me that everybody, if only for a moment, can claim the throne of god.

BATTLE WITHOUT HONOR OR HUMANITY

A black-and-white television that would have passed for a Big Screen in the 1970s sat on a fold-out table in the corner. An extended commercial, or an abbreviated sitcom, called "Shit Calories" played over and over. A bronze-haired adman with a mild case of craniodiaphyseal dysplasia and spraypaint-assisted abs explained that some foods functioned as sheer fuel for the body whereas other foods amounted to dead weight. He emphasized the raging idiocy of non-fat crazes and the revenues gleaned from the healthy fats found in nuts, hummus, salmon, avocados, and various oils. Protein was equally important. "Fuck carbs," he intoned, "barring that which can be extracted from vegetables, small quantities of sweet potatoes, and minuscule quantities of brown rice." He concluded: "Look, it's not hard, you fuckin' fatasses. Anybody can look like me." He stepped back from the camera and bathed in a shower of anabolic rays that enhanced the prowess of his musculature. "Eat like I say and pump iron like a man and you'll get results. Inhale another candy bar and scarf down another bucket of fried chicken and you're nothing but a shiteater. That's shit food, shitheads. Seriously. It's not hard. Eat good and exercise and don't be a fuckin' pussy. That's all you have to do." Before relooping, the adman placed a gun beneath his chin and pulled the trigger.

Some of the Golden Age bodybuilders found inspiration in the adman's coda, enthusiastically grunting through additional reps, whereas others ignored the TV, or stared at it like an alien artifact, uncertain of its capabilities and inborn m.o.

Presidency

An assassin moved across the cracked rubber floor of the gym, handgun pointed at me from an elongated straightarm. He didn't fire, and he didn't run. He walked briskly and assertively, taking long, even strides, and he stared at me with a boxer's fanatic eyes. Reality converged on his approach from multiple angles, moving between closeups of his face, the gun, and his powerful legs, then spinning around his body, obsessively, as if to etch it into an ontology of mourning.

With a cinematic report, the Arab smashed a 25 lb. plate into the assassin's face. The gun flew from his grasp and his feet kicked out in front of him and he went down, hard. A bouquet of blood erupted from the broken gash of his mouth as his head struck the floor. It hung in the air for a moment, a liquid rose, then spread apart like buckshot and spattered a nearby bodybuilder from trapezeus to peroneus, superstylizing the appearance of his grooves better than most affordable tanning sprays.

The Arab appeared to bifurcate into several versions of himself as grim likenesses emerged from the fabric of his bisht and surrounded me. We shot our way out of Gold's Gym, even though we didn't need to—the bodybuilders wanted nothing to do with us—but the Arabs set the dial on Total Bloodshed, and we didn't leave until every musclebound throwback had been put down. Given the means and opportunity, they would have massacred history, too. And they did, after a fashion, murdering a lookalike of Dave Draper, who may have been Dave Draper himself, assuming we had experienced some temporal violation and now inhabited history, a more plausible explanation for this place than the idea that it actually existed in the modern world, and considering Draper's influence on the bodybuilding industry, namely his posthumous deification in virtually every walk of public life, a butterfly effect would ensue and change the course of society and culture, reproducing the future as a potential site of, at the very least, jeopardy and consternation. Convinced we were about to emerge into a new world, I asked for a gun, just to be sure. In thick, jagged accents, the Arabs refused, screaming for me to stay focused and execute the plan.

"Plan," I reiterated.

Outside, everything looked the same—so much so that my escort faded into vague interstices, and when I arrived at headquarters, I felt like a new man. Perhaps the legendary bodybuilder's death had only changed me. That was enough. Solipsism is frowned upon, but in its absence, nothing exists, as everything only exists via the infinitely unique perceptions of individual subjects . . . I might have said that aloud.

"Did I just say something?" I asked a makeup artist.

She shook her head and made a frog face as she dotted my cheeks and neck with oil. "You're a man of few words, Mr. President." There was a happy ending after which I received a guided meditation and scanned my body for nodes of anxiety.

"There are only nodes," I deduced. "Nothing less. No absence. The nodes are the things."

"Let's try again."

We did somewhat better the second time, and I resented dispatching the makeup artist for a moment,

Presidency

despite the pleasure I took in the texture of her skinflesh on my thumbs, the sound of her frail neckbone cracking like an icicle.

The killing incited a mnemonic tempest. I couldn't be sure if what I saw on my mindscreen belonged to me. None of it looked familiar. To my knowledge, I had never killed anybody before, although, like any aspiring Man-of-the-Crowd, I had been working out for years.

. . . Staring at the foregone teleprompter, I waited for the countdown and smoothed out coagulations of fish oil on my arms and chest. Long ago I had concluded that fish oil worked just as well inside the body as it did on the surface. It was as if the substance possessed a magnetic quality that lifted the veins into the air. Of course, no such quality existed; aided by a bit of shine, my vascularity spoke for itself and beckoned even the most sideward attentions.

A grip dealt me the cue with remote fingers: "THREE . . . TWO . . . ONE."

The bulb atop the camera turned green and digitized my image in hi-def monochrome, the format kindest to the nuances of the flesh. Peripherally I saw myself on a makeshift IMAX screen in the corner of the studio. I tried to ignore it.

Contracting my pectoral and abdominal muscles, I read from the teleprompter in a calm, steady, confident, masculine, articulate yet colloquial and casual tone, not too white, not too bourgeois, and occasionally I employed a vague lilt indicating that, behind closed doors, I might not be afraid to express my emotional, essentially feminine core: "My fellow . . . what's that word? Well. Here we stand on the precipice of atrocity. I don't want to remake the country. I want to reestablish its nuclear principles. For instance, I enjoy long walks down aluminum hallways. Additionally, I enjoy skiing in Colorado and arranging women into accordion folders. Sometimes I enjoy being swept away by the absurd delirium of a pop song. I have many memories. One of them involves childhood. I can't be sure but I may have bludgeoned the nextdoor neighbors with a hoe and buried the entire family in my father's garden. Nobody said anything about their disappearance. Years later I became a teenager. I often peered out of the basement window at the garden determined to see things grow if I concentrated hard enough. I have many flaws but my work ethic is truly cosmic and as we all know a cosmic work ethic is essential to the process of identity construction in this country. One day I noticed a bone sticking out of the soil. On the end of it was a shoe. Everybody else noticed it. Nobody said anything. I grew up and here I stand before you today. That's everything. One must always be honest even at the expense of feelings and blood ties. Like everybody I think about a lot of things but mostly my thoughts are preoccupied with groceries and guns. Where to get a good gun. Where to find the bargain prices. So forth. That's honesty. All presidents commit crimes. Some of us get caught and some don't. The real crime is getting caught. Thank you ladies and gentlemen. More on this story as it unfolds."

With a powerful, almost hypnotic (if not rhythmic) crowdstare, I silenced the standing ovation before it had a chance to gain momentum, then went on a minor killing spree, without weapons, since I couldn't seem to get my hands on anything, and I wanted my .357 Colt Python, but I didn't remember what happened to it.

Nor did I remember my name . . .

Confronted by a theoretical maelstrom, the president lifted an empty protein shake container and inspected it. A bead of liquid flowed from the rim. The president wiped it away with a handkerchief . . . and the bead came back, from nowhere.

"The container bleeds," he said gravely. He set it on the desk. "Get me my personal trainer. Now."

The first lady entered the room.

"Who are you?" whirred the president.

She wore a sharp, starched business coat and skirt. Her eyes peered at him from two oilpits of mascara. She said, "Take your clothes off," but he parried the directive and thrust the conversation in a new direction. Soon they were talking about idle trivia.

"Do you remember when you were young? Before the eclipse of corporeality?"

"Sometimes," replied the president.

"Let me refresh your memory."

"Please don't."

"All right. Remember when we used to lie in the sun and fuck like baconwhores? I don't think I cared about anything so much as your Little Elvis back then." She made herself a cosmopolitan on a machine-age cocktail stand as the president reclined in a leather Arlington and surfed through a tolerable selection of channels, blue television light flickering in his eyes. "If only you had cared so much about my privates. Things might have turned out differently. But really it comes down to your first kill. Nothing compared to it. That feeling. Naturally your efforts to reclaim it have been futile. How will your chronic failures be inscribed in the history of your selfhood? I don't know the answer to this question. For now we can only hope for the best and see this term to the end."

"I've never killed anybody." He found a good channel, put aside the remote, and administered an HGH injection between his knuckles with the ease and informality of lighting a cigarette.

The first lady shotgunned the cosmo from a martini glass. "Disgusting," she bleated. She made another one, drank it slower, and said, "I never liked alcohol. I swear I drink it out of habit or something. It's just something I do."

That night, functionally intoxicated, the first lady tucked the president into bed, per usual, and ran fingers down his face—down the forehead, down the nose, down the cheeks and the long, febrile chin—until the contours that defined his body seeped into the mattress and slithered into history.

Battle without Honor or Humanity
Part 1

Exposé

The exhaust fumes of ophicleides and coroners drift across an abandoned playing field. Buoys waver on the sandbar. Spectators are reminded by the Tall Commissar that every word is an artifact of destruction.

Segue to a placid, happy mise-en-scéne depicted with ultraviolent techné.

S/hero

Darla Shine brings the helicopter in low so I can get out. I'm afraid. Somebody has to push me. Shrieking, I fall onto the dolomite floor of the mall and wound my elbow; the skin breaks, bleeds . . . seals and repairs. Darla signals me as she takes the helicopter back up. The long, red hair ebbs and flows in synch with the riptide of her face... My love. My s/hero... Shoppers hurry across the planks and peer over the walkways. The helicopter nears a vaulted glass ceiling. Everybody knows it's going to crash.

Everybody screams as they spill out of the helicopter in slow motion...

This is Boulder, Colorado, circa 2098. Gray mountains hang over the colored, picturesque grid of commerce.

The first body to strike the concrete accomplishes an impossible equation. Ionized tongues of plasma and solar radiation beam into the sky. The other passengers retain their essence, bones shattering like antique windows. Long coils of ink spring out of Darla's eyes and ears. She produces a nightmarish shriek. Dies.

The helicopter goes rogue and breaks the Fourth Wall. It flies into the client's face, stripping flesh from skull, then soars into the clouds, into space, floating, floating, curling around the moon and gaining momentum, and a corona of fire circumscribes the bogie as it penetrates the atmosphere and gravity draws it back to the streets of Boulder... It crashes onto a troupe of lay vorticists, mortally wounding but not killing them. Readers, interpreters and commentators believe the vehicle is disabled, if not destroyed beyond repair. Steam hisses from charred rotors. A mutual sense of complacency sets in... at which point the engine restarts, spinning the heavy blades...

Up in smoke; down the chute—the sinews of grief.

Battle without Honor or Humanity: Part 1

Interrogation

A: And the reason for the advent of your identity?

Angeklagter: I wouldn't call it an advent. I was standing there for, like, a long time. Mostly I just stand around and wait for people to fuck with me. This can take years, assuming I don't resort to dickless provocation. I possess a vast and formidable constitution. I've never met anyone who isn't scared of me. But that doesn't mean nobody picks a fight. Fear is the locomotion of masculinity. Without fear—and insecurity, and idiocy—the male subject wouldn't do anything. He wouldn't get out of bed in the morning to yak in the trash.

B: This is not a matter to be taken lightly.

Angeklagter: I don't take anything lightly. Everything I choose to endure is a cosmic elephant. Frivolity nauseates me. I am not a homunculi. I was born to eat the sky. Look at my face. Look at my eyes. Just one eye. Can you honestly say that my countenance indicates anything other than a healthy entitlement to shit on the entire universe at my leisure? Shreber isn't the only sci-fi god. It's not as if I lack a traumatic kernel. No. My selfhood is empowered by the repressed memories of thousands of pulsing mongrels and chickenbrains. Yes. Yes. Yes. Yes. Yes. That's true. Yes. Invariably I experience a tension between a feeling of genuine happiness and the desire to destroy myself. Let me tell you how it happens. I'll tell you. I get to feeling really goddamn happy—and then I recognize it. What I'm, you know, feeling, I mean. Interpellation is the problem. My happiness calls out to me: "Hey, dipshit, you're happy!" And I realize that I'm susceptible to much more grandiose and devious machinery. Or I simply realize that I'm happy, too happy, and this sort of happiness doesn't last, so I might as well put an end to the fucker now. Depression comes down on me like a Bronze Age anchor. I don't want to kill myself. I've never wanted that. I just want to be tolerated. I just want to exist. Somehow existence must be enough."

X: I have a document that proves you are the owner of the helicopter in question. Is this your signature?

Angeklagter: Document? What document? Did you say document? I don't know what that is. You can't prove my signature is my signature. It is the nature of signatures to evolve with the cult of personality. What looks like my name today could look entirely different tomorrow, or yesterday, or six hundred thousand years ago. I'll tell you something. I am the reincarnation of television's Platonic Form. That cocaine high you get from watching music videos, Stallone movies, Schwarzenegger movies, Van Damme movies—that's me. I am an electromagnetic earthfucker. I have no need for drugs or absinthe. Never have. Van Damme suffered from addiction to El diablo and pussy, I understand. The point is, I am not a man—I am dynamite. I am the Wallace Stegner of the neofabulist world; my Angle of Repose swings between my legs like

Battle without Honor or Humanity: Part 1

a Third World. You may be wondering what I've done to overcome myself today. Nothing. Let me assure you that, in the interests of everyone inscribed by the powers that beleaguer and unman us, the gas tanks of obscurity cry out to the Void like dire infants who have suddenly realized that alienation is the heartbeat of the human condition. Do you know when the heart is ripped out of the chest you can go on living for up to thirty seconds? It must be ripped out quickly, of course, and certain valves must be prepared beforehand for terminal severance. My aorta lies in wait. Dotted lines encircle the fat tentacles in all the right places. Gentlemen, you are barking up the wrong killing spree. I didn't do anything. You don't have anything on me. Am I under arrest? I'm lawyering up. Now. I plan to represent myself. I'm D. Harlan Wilson, Estuary. The D stands for Disambiguation, Dionysis, Defibrillator, Devastation, Diorama, Deli Meat, Dusty "The Amerikan Dream" Rhodes, and *Donaudampfschiffahrtselektrizitätenhaupt*—all at once. I advise my client not to answer any more questions. Let me see that document again. That's not even my client's name. That says Lofton Gitt. I know nothing of this person except that every day is another opportunity for him to adopt and exert the chicaneries of a Slender Man. That's not my client, in any case. Good lord. Can we go now? Are you holding my client here indefinitely? We've answered all of your questions and then some. I demand that you arrest me immediately. The choice is yours. Choice is an illusion, like sky monkeys, but you realize this. Ultimately we don't choose anything. We are chosen. Often against our will. But that is the nature of the cultural maelstrom. We produce culture, extending it from our literal and figurative bodies, and the resultant firmament in turn reproduces us, hurling bolts of mediatized lightning at our souls, imploding the souls. I couldn't tell you what was real and what was fantasy if you had a gun in my mouth. But I'm not trying to run the world, am I? I'm just a cunt on the street. But no, that helicopter doesn't belong to me. I've never seen it before I had this dream. Darla was my wife, though, and I loved her. I was sorry to see her killed.

Interment

The funeral is hard.

Gravediggers don't make a big enough hole and the coffin won't fit. As Reverend Gaylord offers an impromptu eulogy, they climb atop the coffin and try to stomp it into the earth with oversized, untied construction boots, and they keep tumbling onto the grass. They want everything to go smoothly. They are embarrassed by the mistake. But the gravediggers don't know if burial etiquette permits them to return to their shovels and expand the hole during the funeral ceremony.

I make small efforts to help without looking too conspicuous, bending and pushing down on the lid of the coffin, but passing the gesture off as if I have broken into tears, doubled-over, and stopped myself from falling onto my chest.

Battle without Honor or Humanity: Part 1

Elder statesmen glance sternly at me through thick-rimmed photochromic spectacles. Thin, frail mistresses crouch before them in fold-out chairs.

It's no use. Getting the coffin in the hole is like trying to thread a coffee cup through a curtain ring.

Finally Reverend Gaylord completes the eulogy. He apologizes for its directionlessness and the many tangents he pursues, but he has not had ample time to prepare this morning, and he asks for everybody's forgiveness. "Forgiveness is a healthy and essential part of life," he reminds us. "Without it, we would likely be angry all day, every day. Anger isn't a game. Emotions can kill us. Like that." He makes a loud popping sound that alarms half of the crowd. "And emotions come from the brain. So it is our brains that kill us. Do not trust the brain. It does what it wants, and I can only assume that the Devil and Intellect are intimately connected. Kissing cousins, at any rate."

He goes on. Then he politely asks the gravediggers to remove the coffin from the hole, remove the body from the coffin, and place the body in the hole, in the fetal position, to maximize the deficit of space.

Chronicles

The politics of religion descend on Boulder like a flock of buzzards on roadkill. Likewise the religion of politics.

And every sentence ends the same way: . . .

. . . idea for a novel: . . . future-noir of hardnosed hypermasculine urbanites who wear their insecurities on their lapels. No overt satire or silliness. Absurdities of socius, diegesis, etc. must be conveyed with cool-headed gravitas and drama. Incl. slasher film aesthetics? Leave readers with a sense of being robbed and violated. Always.

Notes from the outréground trump the positive aspects of being sick. Sickness is inevitable, but the flu, syphilis, progeria syndrome, etc. don't necessarily predetermine a hauntology of desire. One must adopt psychological armor. There's no other way to negotiate death and the prospect of a terminal conclusion to Mind and Body.

Airfoils sing overhead.

Beneath the music, two demigods battle in the sand.

Anatomy

This is an anatomy of a helicopter, i.e., a rotocraft that may or may not possess multiple propellers. Capable of rising vertically into the sky, defying the laws of physics like a science fictional novum, the helicopter was invented by Etienne Scarpetta, accidentally, and with a certain pejorative finesse, on a bear hunting trip atop Mont Blanc near the border of Switzerland. Inevitably we think of helicopters as timeless marquees of civilization—I have not been surprised when even educated adults have admitted to believing that helicopters predated humanity—but everything possesses (and is dis/possessed by) an origin, except for the unconscious according to Freud, and ideology according to Althusser, and other theories formulated by archeopsychic designers.

Battle without Honor or Humanity: Part 1

... I find myself behind the console. I have placed a photograph of my late wife on the dash. It is vaguely pornographic, but in an endearing way. Splayed out on a motel bed, she wears violet lingerie with black trim and a sleeping mask beneath which hangs a warm off-white smile that seems painted onto her face. I have already begun to forget her. Even as I fly the helicopter, perceive it as an extension of my own body, as a kind of exoskeleton, I realize that I have become obsessed with the machine. But the photograph serves its purpose, and I outmaneuver and outrun my enemies without incident.

I place my hand against the dash and feel the cosmos.

As I land on the roof of my building, I fall asleep at the wheel.

Annotations

I don't know how to account for the growing popularity of postcapitalists other than to suggest that the future enables their errant behavior and subsequent mass appeal.

We may contextualize the future by remembering the past. We remember the past by reimagining the future.

As stated by my dead co-pilot: "In the cold courts of justice the dull head demands oaths, and holy writ proofs, but in the warm halls of the heart one single, untestified memory's spark shall suffice to enkindle such a blaze of evidence, that all the corners of conviction are suddenly lighted up as a midnight city by a burning building, which on every side whirls its reddened brands."

BATTLE WITHOUT HONOR OR HUMANITY

The best way to treat grief is to multiply it by epic proportions/proposals. One quantity of grief hurts; one hundred thousand quantities transcend the spectrum of agony. Too much of a bad thing doesn't work. You get to a certain point and everything goes numb. I propose the anaphoric multiplication of my epic pain.

Then it is mourning again.

If only every fleeting phase of the day could be like the yellow mourning.

When your tears flow across the empty boulevard. When ontology makes grim sense. When you know who you are and where you're going.

Never use the second person in formal writing.

Lebensmittelgeschäfte

Fish oil. *Desodorierendes Mittel.*

Interlocution

I exclaim, "I can't stop thinking about it. It keeps running through my head. It's all I can think about."

"Shut the fuck up."

I have gone to the movies again. A bloody action s/hero film. The theater is at full capacity, rife and waterlogged, and I have secured an aisle seat. I have not purchased a soda. I have not purchased candy or popcorn.

Ushers guard the emergency exits with their lives.

Battle without Honor or Humanity: Part 1

I exclaim, "I know I won't always feel this way. I experience chronic mood swings. I wouldn't go so far as to call myself bipolar. But I'd call myself something. Sometimes I feel like the actor Timothy Olyphant—gifted, good-looking, Hawaiian, underrated, in some cases altogether unknown. That reminds me. My father encased my legs in prosthetic technologies. I don't recall anything being wrong with me. I think his intention was to test and examine the technologies. I do recall tripping quite a bit. I recall breaking bones, too. I died, once."

"Hey. Asshole. Shut the fuck up."

I can tell by the sound of his voice that he's big.

I exclaim, "I am an electric samurai. I am the noblest savage. I am precisely what I want to be. I slay cumulonimbus clouds with one hand, oceans with the other. I colonize the Giant Places. And yet failure lurks around every corner. It has been said that I heave entire diegeses from the bowels of my action-painter's bucket like a magician yanking a syphilitic kangaroo from a ten gallon hat. But the scope of my intentions transcends my great remove. The universe cannot hold me accountable for these deeds, these breaches of gestalt. These wild therapies. The world is my analysand and my conclusion is that the world should place Barrel against Temple and blow Brains against Empty White Canvass. I have never owned a gun, but I have fired guns, on occasion. As a child on the prairie—bored, alone, deranged—I spent my afternoons picking off squirrels, finches, lizards, and other godless creatures with my father's .22 rifle. They exploded like mortal fireworks. This was in the

BATTLE WITHOUT HONOR OR HUMANITY

Boy Scouts. I made it to Eagle Scout and soared into the heavens only so I could discharge shitbombs onto the hungry watchers. I have a confession to make. I was the Human Beat Box in the rap group the Fat Boys. The way it worked: Crazy White Boy plus Black Fat Suit equals Human Beat Box. His death by heart attack—a grand and terrific hoax. Now here we are. I don't mean to be glib, or impractical. Never. I only do the best I can to convey my perspective, to extend my selfhood, and to negotiate the various ways in which I am interpellated by countless Ideological State Apparatuses. This movie stinks. I don't believe the antagonist means it when s/he kills somebody."

As blood splashes artfully across the camera lens, blocking the audience's view of a gruesome wound, I feel his hand on my shoulder, and I shoot out of my seat like a broken clockspring.

We collide.

We exchange blows.

We set reality on fire.

Rolling across the treacherous swill, we engage in a battle without honor or humanity.

Boycott

I go to a free-range boycott with my sponsor. He insists that I "introject" myself into the "public veinscape" on a regular basis. I tell him that he's using "introject" improperly—as a verb and as a concept. It's not raining

Battle without Honor or Humanity: Part 1

and the stars are out, but I see storm clouds rolling in from the sidebars, and I hear the arthritic moans of distant thunder.

Now I am in Fort Wayne, Indiana. Colorado belongs to my fever dreams, my delirium tremens.

I run a finger across a brick wall. Ceramic flakes fall onto my knuckles and into my palm.

It is 2015 again.

I don't know what's being boycotted. An angry crowd has gathered in front of a medical textbook store. My sponsor and I get close to the crowd so that we can hear what everybody's talking about.

They're talking about glands.

Glands, in fact, is what they are boycotting, staging the affair outside of a pawnshop that deals in books about glands, among other superfluities. Glands are overrated, they say. Glands are myths, they say. We as a society have been trained to think that glands are indispensable for human existence when the truth of the matter is they are largely unnecessary and in many cases inimical. This veil of illusions must be lifted. And somebody must pay.

The one gland they make a concerted exception for is the breast. The many glands that constitute the breast. They serve a very real purpose, actually and figuratively. The latter in particular. Several participants tote signs with crudely illustrated pictures of impossible breasts on them. Chickenscratch solar coronas encircle the breasts. Arching above them is the acronym ADNI (Artifacts of Desire Not Included).

BATTLE WITHOUT HONOR OR HUMANITY

In an unobtrusive frenzy, I realize that the participants belong to a certain variety of bald, withered men defined by catastrophic pejorativity.

It starts to rain.

My sponsor walks me through the five stages of grief, otherwise known as the Kübler-Ross model: denial, anger, bargaining, depression, acceptance—in that precise order. I explain that I have been experiencing the stages backwards. I accepted Darla Shine's death immediately; it was very much a relief, since I often obsessed about death, especially the death of loved ones, how much it would hurt when it happened, when it would happen, then the loneliness, the self-pity, the fear of consciousness being extinguished forever, shattered like a Tiffany lamp, etc., so when that helicopter killed Darla, who I had loved more than any other woman (and I had loved many other women), I was almost happy—I accepted it like an envelope of crisp, untraceable $100 bills. Then I slipped into a deep depression because I realized I shouldn't have accepted her death so willfully, so comfortably. I started to bargain with myself. If you get a little sadder about Darla, I told myself, you won't be so depressed, not about not being depressed because of Darla anyway. I countered the offering with a general truth: Depression is a phantasmagoria made flesh by ways of seeing. I went back and forth with myself. Time passed. This made me angry, my battle. And deranged. I told myself that I wasn't angry and deranged, even though I clearly was. Hence denial. Then I felt calm. Hence the end of the five stages of grief—backwards.

Battle without Honor or Humanity: Part 1

My sponsor squeezes my elbow and says, "It's all right to cry." I tell him I know that but I don't feel like crying. He lobbies to convert me into a monograph. I cock my head like the hammer of a six-shooter.

"Glands," whispers a stranger. He raises a sleep-jagged brow ... and his pale face derails, sliding into collisions of meaning and usurpation.

Mnemonics

I forget about helicopters. I see pictures of them in books. I see them fly overhead in migratory regiments.

I don't know what they are.

Hypertension

They say my blood pressure has "matriculated" from the "confectionary" to the mildly "astrofuturistic." Last reading: 110/70. Today's reading: 600/422. "Thus," chirps the Chief Executive of Hôpital Saint Cognée, "I introduce you to middle age and the registration of certain armorial bearings. Cirrhosis crouches on the horizon like a starved leopard; a fist of scars squeezes the liver into submission and the vital juices cease to flood the mainstream. I shall prescribe you a heaving quantity of lisinopril-hydro-chlorithiazide alongside unlimited stores of Xanax and Lorazepam. Beware addiction. Beware the tides of desire. Beware consciousness. Beware life and everyone in it. Or seek out more constructive and accepting pastures. Given these numbers, you are not alive. Savor every moment. Every new day is a rift."

I escape Paris in a steam dummy.

I scan my body with *dhyānaic* rigor and explore my symptoms . . . shortness of breath . . . heart palpitations . . . fatigue . . . rage . . . more rage . . . delusions of persecution sublimated into cosmic opulence . . . and regret. Empathy for the Devil. I embrace a phantom pathology that ushers me through a maze of reason. Blood wells up in my eyes and surges down my cheeks. I cover the lesions with authentic Elvis sunglasses. They are the same sunglasses Christian Slater brandishes in *True Romance* (1993), with dark, vast, alien-eye lenses and thick, gold, bullet-hole rims.

Grindhouse

Fort Wayne defies urbanity. Population: 10 million troglodytes. Most of them live underground in provisional meth labs and Cold War bomb shelters and rarely come up for air. The overworld itself consists of a YMCA, a building with a broken rotating restaurant on the roof, a used bookstore, and a grassless park punctuated by rusty jungle gyms. It is boderline postapocalyptic, in theory, although not as foreboding as Lima, Ohio, or Gary, Indiana, the industrial wastelands of which make Fort Wayne look like Candyland. Such hideous vistas transcend the glands and constitute the very definition of beauty and legend.

Battle without Honor or Humanity: Part 1

Lacunae

I remember when I told Darla Shine that I wanted to become a rockstar. "It's a prosaic desire," I said, eyes like kamikaze moon rocks. "But I can do it."

It took me about two weeks. I did some research the following morning, and in the evening I wrote eleven and a half songs—the average number on every Journey album with Steve Perry as frontman. I entitled the halfsong "A Slice of Rapture." The full revision process took about twenty minutes, including toilet and coffee breaks. The songs, I hoped, accomplished a dynamic stupidity that would be easily misinterpreted by molten intellects as dramatic ingenuity, rendering their composer an architect of the soul. Of course, I had always possessed a luminous voice fit for the Arena. Since the age of five, I spoke in a cavernous baritone, harrowing my peers with threats of certain manhood. My singing voice is a different animal. By my calculations, my vocal range runs the gamut from bass low F to coloratura falsetta F-natural, and I'm capable of achieving heights the likes of tenor high F in my belting register. Coupled with an unmitigated creativity fueled by megalomania and hypermasculinity, I could have become a rockstar at any moment in my life following the dawn of chest hair. I simply elected not to do so . . . until now. And now there's no going back.

By way of random crank calls, I herded together a percussionist, a bassist, etc. I invited them over and we introduced ourselves formally and then got fucked up. We discovered an advertisement for a record label on a milk carton and secured a contract within hours, just as the shakes set in. We smoked hundreds of thousands of cigarettes. We practiced a few songs, then got fucked up again and headed into the studio. We winged it. A few days later I heard "A Slice of Rapture" on the radio. One week later I was punching and roundhousing excited fans off of one stage after another. Girls. Girls. Girls. Tropicana's where I lost my heart. This went on for about ten years. At the apex of our career, I established a kind of cult religion requiring devotees to essentially steal entire sitting booths from chain restaurants and "retire them to the hollow earth." I rarely saw Darla, but she didn't divorce me, and when it was over, I slipped back into my role as if I had never achieved stardom, detoxing in a matter of seconds by sheer mental effort, and finally reconfiguring my evolved worldview, which changed considerably with the onslaught and rise of celebrity consciousness. Misanthropy eluded me and I reverted to a guiltless state of rest. It was a boring miracle.

Optics

There's a scene in *Snow White & the Seven Dwarves* (1937), near the beginning, where the Queen orders a huntsman to kill the *femme nature*. The huntsman doesn't want to do it, but he's scared of the Queen, so he goes into the woods where Snow White is singing songs with birds.

The hunstman takes out a knife and sneaks up behind her. He steps on a twig.

Battle without Honor or Humanity: Part 1

Startled, Snow White glances over her shoulder and we see the reflection of her widening eyes in the blade ...

"My daughter consistently misreads the scene," I explain, "thinking the huntsman's intent is not to murder her, but rather to measure her eyes. She neither cares nor knows what for. The knife thus emerges as an instrument of optical calculation intended either to improve or disprove Snow White's quality of life."

A voice the likes of the Magic Mirror, cavernous and dreamy, replies to me from the rafters, the sewers: "You don't have a daughter. You never have. Additionally, that's not how it happens. The huntsman doesn't step on a twig. As he creeps towards her, his shadow grows and swallows Snow White, and she gets wise to the darkness behind her. Something else. We don't see her reflection in the blade. And her eyes barely crack a smile, in a manner of speaking. It is the huntsman's eyes that inflate like kamikaze moon rocks and burn brightly with fear and self-loathing for being a coward and not standing up to the Queen."

"The Queen!" cries Snow White ...

Darwinism

Big Thoughts on the philosophy of coaching a competitive sport ... And suddenly I am the coach. Rancorous. Balding. Christian. Republican. A spool of flab hanging over the belt ... I don't care how young the players are: crow's feet are mandatory during prayer. We stack hands and pray to the lord for a win. We pray again for our sins to be forgiven so that we can win. We pray again for a big fucking win. We continue to pray. "Lord," my lips utter, "let us buttfuck our opponents harder than they've ever been buttfucked before. Please. Please, lord." I am whispering now. "Let us tear their asses apart with our giant, begotten, fuck-everything-that-moves cocks." There is a devout pause during which my pursed lips twitch and then deliver a commanding "Amen." The players open their eyes. I look at them, at their faces, their eyes, and I decide we need to pray some more. We kneel and lock arms, cutting off the circulation of blood to our forearms and hands. The limbs swell and turn purple as I intone: "Please, please, we must eviscerate every last dirty son of a bitch..."

Autobiographika

Mustard attack. The residual smell haunts me. We used to eat them like figs, plucking them straight from the vine. They tasted unnatural, inorganic.

We drive to a wine bar in a strip mall next door to a TJ Maxx. It offers the most compelling atmosphere in the city, and the service is good to boot. Fort Wayne's cultural elite stride manfully between the paper-clothed tables in steam-ironed suits.

My date stares at me firmly, yet quizzically, uncertain about my intentions and her desires. She has put on too much makeup and seems ashamed of it. She has concealed

Battle without Honor or Humanity: Part 1

her cleavage and seems to regret it. She drums a finger against the table as if testing a new hi-hat.

"I've been writing my memoirs," I explain to her. It's the first date I've been on since the murder. Or accidental death. My memory continues to defy and utterly defeat me. History is a shin splint."

"Memoirs?" she blurts. "Who's gonna read them? Who are they for?"

"Nobody. Me. Everybody."

She takes a sip of wine and makes a face.

"You must have an exciting life." She signals a waiter. "What're they about?" She arbitrates a false innuendo. "The memoirs."

I try to process what's happening and say, "Various dreamscapes and happenings. Mostly absolute truths."

A waiter passes by like skinned carrion in an abattoir.

"That doesn't sound very interesting." She removes an initialed handkerchief from her purse and quietly blows her nose.

"It's not, really. They're not, I mean. The memoirs." I repeat the word in my head. "It's a matter of elocution. How I say things. How I write them."

"So you lie, basically." She inspects the dirty handkerchief, unable to negotiate its condition.

I say, "I guess. Basically, I guess."

Something occurs to me. Noxious efforts to disarm the night.

No. Something else.

Frowning, she reluctantly feeds the handkerchief to the purse. "That sounds mean. Dumb, too."

BATTLE WITHOUT HONOR OR HUMANITY

Later, at my $800,000 home, we make rough love in the master bedroom, slipping into our respective roles as mediatized sex objects like veteran synthespians.

Bubonic

De facto embodiment: I find myself holding a samurai sword, the leather handle long and grooved and worn, but somehow inviolate, and I maneuver the weapon with a totem of two glued fists. I allow my opponent to put me on the defense. I draw him in, and then I bow to one side, devoutly, presciently, softening my elbows, editing the coalescence of my shoulder muscles, and finally sweeping upwards in an act of sociopathic, hate-fueled cathexis. My breath leaves my esophagus like the exhaust fumes of a luxury vehicle as the tip of the blade passes through my opponent's face. It doesn't touch the upper teeth or the palate. It splits the chin, the jawbone and the tongue. When he falls to his knees in the dust, and when his mouth drops open and apart like an exploded mine shaft, the tongue flails in the screaming wound like two bubonic snakes.

Ubiquity

My soul goes viral.

I relinquish it from the prison of my ribcage.

The soul floods innerspace and gains momentum and girth like a scintillating blob of reckoning.

Battle without Honor or Humanity: Part 1

Within days: ubiquity.

I am a Hollow Man. I am the Forever Man. I conjure narratives of superheroes and skylords and my synapses snap to attention like fallen Lucifers.

A shriveled husk stands tall on the portal.

And nothing's changed. I feel the same way I felt when my bird was caged, gladly, its beak sealed shut with an iron barrette, its outlook riddled by unburied desires, by time and experience and basement-going.

Conclusion: godliness is next to emptiness.

Revision: there are no glands on the surface of the enframed body...

Admission: free of charge. But you will learn nothing and be required to excel.

Battle without Honor or Humanity

Silhouette of a boy, thin and awkward as a flayed pike, playing in the reeds...

The sun goes down.

The boy plucks a cattail from the marsh and holds it overhead, pretending it's a torch that will light his way through the drama.

BATTLE WITHOUT HONOR OR HUMANITY

D. HARLAN WILSON is a novelist, short story writer, editor, literary critic, playwright, and Professor of English at Wright State University-Lake Campus. In addition to over twenty works of fiction and nonfiction, hundreds of his stories and essays have appeared in magazines, journals and anthologies throughout the world in multiple languages. Wilson serves as reviews editor for *Extrapolation*, editor-in-chief of Anti-Oedipus Press, and managing editor of Guide Dog Books.

www.DHarlanWilson.com
www.TheKyotoMan.com

Printed in August 2022
by Rotomail Italia S.p.A., Vignate (MI) - Italy